LIGHTNING RIDERS

A Clay Jared Western

R. Annan

Lightning Riders
Copyright 2016 by R. Annan
WGA Reg. #: R31694 (1.12.16)

Author's Portrait by Hazel Tertsakian
Editor: Karren Doll Tolliver
Photography © L. Annan

One Vision Publishing
ISBN: 978-1-942338-50-5 (eBook)
ISBN: 978-1-942338-49-9 (Print)

Other western books by R. Annan:
Fight for The Lazy M
The Red Bandana
The Gunfighter in Winter
Long Ride to Hell's Kitchen
Owl Hawks
Gunfight at Barfield Springs
Shootout at Sanctuary City
Last Days of a Gunfighter
Copperhead Moon
Cowboys of the Box R
Prisoners of Brimstone Pass
Range War in C Minor
Devil Wind
Showdown at Wamego Falls

To

L.A, J.A. and T.A.

You know who you are!

1.

Six men rode through the night. A full moon showed they wore hoods and carried guns. One also carried an unlit torch. As they plowed through a field of high switch grass, their horses kicked up plumes of dew droplets that danced like silver sparks in the moonlight.

They followed their leader up a rise. At the top, he waved them to a stop and signaled to them to spread out.

Below, clear in the moonlight, was a small sod house, a lean-to and a buckboard. Farming equipment lay scattered about the yard. Across from the lean-to was a pigpen and a chicken coop. A horse stood sleeping in the lean-to. Behind all this were rows of corn and other vegetables. These crops were enclosed with a three-strand barbed-wire fence and a gate.

The windows of the house were dark.

The farm was carved out of a section of lush rangeland. Outside, near the fence, cattle stood motionless in large groups. Rich grazing grass stretched like an ocean of green for miles in all directions. A long, thin dirt road was connected to the farm. It led to a town several miles away and was like an umbilical cord, a lifeline for those who lived on the farm.

At this late hour no one in the house was awake. A mangy old dog was tied to a tree stump near the door. It lay curled up in a ball, sleeping soundly.

The leader turned his horse to the right and rode down the hill to a tall oak tree. The others followed. They sat there staring at the rows of tall, green young corn waving in the night breezes. The stalks made a whispering sound.

Two of the riders slipped quietly to the ground and walked to the fence. They took a pair of wire cutters from their back pockets and quickly cut a section of fence loose. After that, they lifted the entire section out of the ground, carried it into the yard and laid it down.

Just as the dog came awake and started to bark, two more riders rode in and looped their lariats around the loose section of fence. Seconds later they raced off into the cornfield, dragging the section of fence behind them, knocking down three rows of corn at a time. While this was happening, the rest of the men followed the leader into the yard.

One man rode to the chicken coop and one to the pigpen. They both started firing into the animals. The man with the torch lit it and set fire to the lean-to. Another rider joined him and shot the horse.

Screams of terror came from the pigpen, the chicken coop and the lean-to. Pigs charged the pen fence and piled up in a heap as the night riders poured shot after shot into them. The chickens were shot in midair as they tried to escape. Soon the smell of burning meat and feathers rose in the air.

A shot rang out. A man in overalls stood in the doorway of the house with an old shotgun, cursing. As he stopped to reload, the leader fanned off three shots. The man dropped the gun, clutched his heart and fell dead in a heap before the door of his house. The leader then shot the dog.

Sounds of children crying came from the house. A baby's high-pitched wail echoed in the crisp night air. Someone inside was barricading the door.

"Shall we finish 'em, boss?" one of the riders asked.

"No," the leader said, putting his gun away. "Let's go help the others."

They turned their horses around and rode into the rows of green, trampling down crops and uprooting newly planted apple and plum saplings. Swinging their lariats, they tore through the farmland like a whirlwind, cutting down everything in their path. An hour later the leader decided they had done enough damage and called his men in.

They gathered together and left.

The moon followed them as they rode like demons across long stretches of grazing land. In another hour they arrived at their destination, the yard of the Diamond C Ranch. Heading down to the barn, they quickly dismounted and tended to their horses. Finally, after putting the animals in the corral, they walked slowly towards the darkened bunkhouse.

"If any of the other boys git nosey, tell 'em ta talk to me," the leader told the five men. They nodded and filed into the bunkhouse.

The leader stopped in front of the ranch house porch. A man stood there hidden in the shadows.

"How did it go, Larkin?" the man asked. He spoke low.

"We had a little problem, Mr. Carter," Larkin replied, also keeping his voice low but just above a whisper.

"Serious?" the man asked as he lit a match. The light revealed a round, delicate but stern looking face with small, black eyes. A cigar hung from his mouth. He lit it and blew the match out.

"Yes," the man called Larkin replied.

There was a brief silence and the man called Carter said, "I see. Alright, then, maybe you had best stop for a while."

"You think so, sir?"

"Yes. We've done three raids already this month. Maybe we should slack off. Someone might get suspicious and start pointing fingers."

"Alright, Mr. Carter, if that's what you want. At least we've taught those nesters who's boss in the valley, sir," Larkin said.

"Yes, we have," Carter replied.

"What about the small ranchers?" Larkin asked.

"We'll lay off them for a while, too."

"We've got them on the ropes, you know. A few more hits and they're done for."

Carter thought about that.

"I know, but I'm thinking of another way to finish them off."

"Oh?"

"Yes, maybe I can get Addison to do the dirty work for us. He's got problems with the small ranchers, too."

"The railroad man? Yeah. That would be good, if you could pull that off."

Carter nodded. The conversation was finished. He went into the ranch house and Larkin went into the bunkhouse.

"Is that you, dear?" a woman's voice asked.

"Yes, my love."

"It's late. Come to bed."

"Alright, my sweet."

Carter went upstairs to bed.

2.

Evil needs company. By itself, it shrivels up and dies. That's why Lane Carter needed Stern Addison. They were both evil men.

Lane Carter sat in a plush chair in the Cattlemen's Association Building sipping a glass of bourbon and reading *The Thompson Gulch Valley Star*. The editorial read:

> "Two days ago, a band of night riders attacked the ranch of Seth Rooney, killing him and destroying much of his property as well as his crops. It was a cowardly deed carried out by unknown forces."

It went on:

> "Who would do such a thing as that? Who benefits by this? Each person who reads this editorial must ask himself that same question. Who did this awful thing? I think we all know!"

Carter chuckled and set the paper down. His Diamond C Ranch was the biggest in Thompson Gulch Valley. His over 300,000-acre spread grazed over 150,000 head of prime beef. His cows were purebreds descended from the Texas Longhorn paired with Brown Swiss and Ayrshire stock.

The result was, however, they didn't have quite the staying power and strength of the Longhorn. Good graze and abundant water was the key to their survival on the Kansas plains. And the nesters and small ranchers were using most of that up.

Carter wasn't going to let that go on any longer. He figured it was time to put an end to the nesters and small ranchers once and for all.

Since the railroad was key to Carter's operation, he was a big investor. In fact, he had met Jay Gould, the railroad magnate, himself. Carter also cultivated connections with the local agent of the Kansas Pacific Railroad, a man named Stern Addison. The result was that he got reduced shipping rates, saving him thousands of dollars.

As for the smaller ranchers in the area, they had to suffer higher shipping costs than did Carter, and that made them very angry. They both detested and hated the big rancher. Few of them, if any, ever attended the Cattlemen's Association monthly meetings because Carter was always there to gloat and smirk at them.

Carter also had political influence in the state capital and was on the board of the Cattlemen's Savings and Loan in town as well.

But the farmers, once seen by the small ranchers as nesters and sodbusters, soon became their friends. In an effort to fight back against Carter, the small ranchers joined forces with the farmers to form the Granger Savings and Loan Bank.

Early on, the farmers and the small ranchers found out that the railroad was not their friend. It granted favors to Carter and the other big ranchers, but not to them. The railroad, being a government supported monopoly, could pretty much do as it wanted. The farmers, especially, had no other options than to pay the higher prices. That or let their crops rot on the station platform.

The Kansas Pacific Railroad agent assigned to the Thompson Gulch area was a man called Stern Addison. He was especially good at breaking railroad strikes and had had a hand in breaking the great railroad strike of 1886 by hiring professional gunman to bust up the strikers.

Jay Gould, the wealthy railroad magnate, was rumored to have said, "I can hire half of the working class to kill the other half."

Carter and Addison were two men of the same mind as Gould. They did whatever it took to solve the problem at hand, no matter who got hurt in the process.

Addison, especially, had connections with certain men who did what was asked of them as long as the money was right. Men who didn't care who got hurt. To them it was all about money.

One such man was Edward Stryker. Addison had often used him sparingly to take care of people who got in the way of railroad operations. Stryker was a freelancer and liked to keep hidden in the shadows. He'd come out when given a task to his liking. He was particular in that respect and didn't jump at just any offer.

"If you need Ed Stryker, let me know," Stern Addison often told Carter. "I'll send for him. But the offer has to be good. He won't take any old thing you throw at him. He's strictly his own man."

"I'll keep that in mind," Carter replied.

Addison rented a room at the hotel in Thompson Gulch, but conducted his private business in a plush V.I.P. railroad car fifty yards away from the train depot and telegraph office. The room was luxuriously furnished with a small bedroom and a well-stocked bar. Carter was a regular visitor.

One day Addison said to Carter, "Look, Carter, if you could get your hands on all the land in the valley, I could convince the bigwigs in Kansas City to put a spur right down the center all the way to Larchmont Springs. You'd wind up a very rich man. But, of course, I'd want a cut."

"How much?"

"Say, forty-five percent," Addison replied.

Carter sneered. "You're dreaming, Addison. Fifteen percent is as high as I'll go."

Addison came back with a quick counter offer.

"Twenty-percent. You'd get a town named after you. Carterville. You'd be famous."

Carter considered that and was instantly hooked.

"Alright, then, twenty percent," Carter replied.

Carter congratulated himself on getting the number down to where he wanted it. He had beaten Addison down from forty-five to twenty percent. He chuckled.

"What's the joke, Carter?" Addison asked.

"Oh, nothing."

Suddenly Addison was smiling, too, and Carter wondered why. Had he missed something? Did Addison know something he didn't?

What he didn't know was that Addison would get a hefty finder's fee from the railroad upon completion of the deal. That fee would amount to twenty percent of the value of the land. Addison, in effect, would be getting twenty percent from Carter and another twenty percent from the railroad for a total of forty percent. He, too, would be a rich man. Carter hadn't put anything over on him like he thought he had.

A few days after their discussion about the land, Carter rode his buckboard into town one evening to see Addison at the V.I.P. car. Since the bedroom end was usually locked, Carter entered, without knocking, through the other end where the bar was. He didn't see Addison, so he called out.

"Anybody home?"

"Be right out!"

He heard noises and muffled voices in the back room. One was feminine. After a few moments Addison came out straightening his clothes. His face was flushed red. When Carter saw it, he laughed.

"Did I come at a bad time, Addison?"

"Ah, no," Addison said, panting.

He walked to the bar, poured a shot of whiskey for himself and sat down in a plush chair by the window to drink. Without being asked, Carter took a chair facing him. He wondered why Addison was acting so strange, as if he were guilty of something.

Addison inhaled to catch his breath then cleared his throat.

"So, what brings you into town, Carter?" he asked.

Carter glanced back towards the bedroom door.

"Are you sure I didn't interrupt something," Carter teased. He enjoyed making Addison feel uncomfortable.

"I said no!" Addison snapped.

Carter chuckled. Addison seemed on edge.

"About that man, that, what's his name? The one who fixes problems? You know who I mean?"

"Yes," Addison said. "Ed Stryker. What about him?"

"I'd like to talk to him."

"What about?"

"A job I have in mind."

"Are you sure?"

"Yes. Why?"

"He doesn't like people to waste his time. You either have a job or you don't."

"Well, I do."

"Alright, then, I'll send him a wire to meet you here."

"Okay, good," Carter said.

Addison glanced nervously at the bedroom door.

"Is that all?" He seemed anxious to have Carter leave.

"Yes," Carter said and stood up. He purposely stared back at the bedroom door again to see Addison's reaction.

"If that's all, I have some business to attend to," Addison said.

"Of course," Carter said. "Let me know when Stryker gets here, won't you?"

"I said I would. Goodnight," Addison said coldly.

Outside, as he rode away in his buckboard, Carter chuckled. He had evidently interrupted Addison at a delicate and embarrassing moment.

He wondered who the girl was. He'd have to find out. Maybe he could use it against Addison someday.

You never could tell about those things.

3.

"What took you so long, Stryker?" Carter asked.

He and Addison were seated in the V.I.P. car staring up at the man called Stryker who stood leaning casually against the bar with a glass of whiskey in his left hand.

Stryker was just over six feet tall, lean and muscular, dressed all in black except for his leather vest. His Stetson was tilted back just enough to show his handsome, clean-shaven face. His right hand hung down by his Colt more out of habit than anything else.

"What the hell took you so long, Stryker?" Carter asked again.

"I had to say goodbye to a friend." Stryker's voice had that rich Texas twang to it.

"A whole week?" Carter asked sharply.

"She was special," Stryker chuckled.

Carter tried to outstare the new arrival, to show him who was boss. It didn't work too well.

"So, what's the deal?" Stryker asked as if he really didn't care all that much.

"Come over here and I'll tell you," Carter said, pointing to a chair nearby. He had just given Stryker an order. Stryker shrugged. He took his time walking over and sitting down.

"I've got nesters," Carter said. It was as if he was admitting to having lice.

Stryker asked. "Is that all?"

"No, I've got ranchers, too. Small ones, who have sided with the nesters."

Stryker laughed.

"What's so funny?" Carter asked.

"I've heard this story before. A hundred times. It goes like this," Stryker said. "It's a very simple plot. You want their land and they won't sell. You made the offer and they refused. Now you're pissed off and can't wait any longer."

"There's more to it," Carter replied. "The wire those nesters put up kill my special bred cows and bulls, and they're plowing up all the grass. And the small ranchers are rustling my beef. I want an end put to it."

"To them."

"What?"

"You want an end put to them, not it."

Carter stared at Stryker thinking he wasn't so dumb.

"Well, isn't that your line of work? That's what you do for a living, isn't it?"

Now they were down to brass tacks. Now they could talk business.

"Yes, that's what I do," Stryker replied. "So, what do you want done?"

"First, I want you to make it so the small ranchers sell. Most of them are in trouble at the bank so I'll get first bid."

"You got a connection with the bank, I take it?"

"That's not your concern. Your job is to make life so hard for the ranchers they'll be glad to sell."

"What about the nesters?"

"Don't worry about them. That part is covered. I just want you to work on the ranchers first. Make sure they fold."

"Sure," Stryker said. "You'll have to point them out to me. Can you do that?"

"There's a fundraiser coming up for the widow of a nester named Seth Rooney who got killed two weeks ago," Carter explained. "It's over in the Grange Hall, outside town. We'll show up and make a donation. I'll point out the ones I want taken care of."

The gunman shrugged. "Sure, whatever you say."

"Okay, now let's talk money," Carter said.

Stryker nodded. "Sure. How about a thousand a head?"

Carter was ready for that and had his own figure in mind.

"Too much. Five hundred or it's no deal."

"Then it's no deal," Stryker said and stood up. He turned to Addison "It's been nice meeting you, Mr. Addison." He turned and walked slowly towards the door.

"Damn it, wait!" Carter yelled. Stryker knew he had his man. Carter needed him badly. "Alright, a thousand a head, then."

Stryker stopped and turned around.

"One thing," Carter said. "You can't dress like that when you're with me."

Stryker chuckled. "Sure. I have a suit."

"Then wear it," Carter said as if chastising a child.

"Give me five hundred," Stryker said suddenly.

"What?"

"I said give me five hundred."

"Why?"

"In case you get cold feet and decide to change your mind, is why."

"You want it now?"

"Yes."

Carter grudgingly got the money out of his billfold and handed it to Stryker.

He had a sudden dislike for this obstinate man.

4.

A lone cowboy stopped at a stream outside the town of Thompson Gulch and let his horse drink. When the animal was finished, the cowboy rode up a rise and stopped to look down. He saw a sprawling cattle town attached to a railroad that ran east and west like a lifeline. All around the town there were herds of cattle feeding on plush grazing land. Cattle stretched for as far as the eye could see. Cowboys, like tiny ants, rode guard on the herds.

The cowboy also caught the flash of barbed wire in the afternoon sunlight. Inside the wire there were small nester farms that ate into the cattle land. Thin dirt roads snaked out from the farms and attached themselves to a wide coach road. The coach road, which was the main artery, ran for miles east and west until it disappeared behind the horizon in both directions.

Hooking one leg around the saddle horn, the cowboy took out his tobacco and casually rolled a cigarette. He lit it and smoked while examining the scene around him. He seemed to be in no hurry. His horse chomped at the tall grass that spread all around.

When the animal finished eating, the cowboy got it headed down the slope towards the town. When he arrived, he rode slowly up the main street, avoiding people who crisscrossed busily in front of him. As he came to a place called the Blue Steer Saloon, he stopped to consider going in or down to the stockyards.

A flip of the coin decided the matter. He tied up and went into the saloon.

It looked and smelled like every saloon in every cattle town he had ever been in. It had a warped plank bar, worn tables and beat-up chairs. Oil lamps hung from the rafters above, and a huge mirror and a selection of local beer and whiskey sat behind the bar.

It made the cowboy feel right at home.

Since it was a Friday, some of the townsfolk and a few cowboys stood at the bar talking and drinking. Others were at the tables playing cards.

"I'm Ted. What'll it be, cowboy?" the barman said as the cowboy came up to lean on it. Ted's eyes did a quick survey of the newcomer. He knew most faces in the area. Sooner or later every cowpoke in the valley came into the Blue Steer Saloon. They told him more about themselves than he cared to know.

The cowboy smiled and looked past him to the cluster of bottles lined up on the sideboard in front of the mirror. There was a selection of red eye and beer.

"What's good?" The cowboy nodded towards the mirror.

"We've got some good local brews. Take yer pick."

The cowboy scratched his chin and stared at the collection of beers.

"How about that one in the green bottle. Is it any good?"

"Skull Buster? It ain't bad. Bitter as hell, though."

"I can handle bitter, as long as it's wet."

As the barman reached for the green flip-top, the cowboy took note of the jars of hardboiled eggs in brine, pickled cucumbers, beef jerky and hardtack lined up on the counter in front of the mirror. He asked for two eggs, a pickle, a piece of jerky and a piece of hardtack.

"The hardtack is free," the barman said as he tossed it all on a chipped plate. He set it in front of the cowboy. "Be careful, though, it'll break yer teeth."

The cowboy chuckled and put a double eagle on the bar.

"Yer new around here, aincha?" Ted asked.

"Yep."

"Lookin' fer work?"

"Yep," the cowboy said with a mouthful. He demolished the eggs as if he hadn't eaten in a week.

"Well, you don't wanna look here." The barman said. It sounded like a warning.

"How come?"

"Bad things are going on. Somebody is trying ta wipe out the nesters an' ranchers."

"Really? Who? Why?"

The bartender's face took on an intense glare. He squinted mysteriously and spoke in a whisper.

"Thet's one question ya don't ask around here, cowboy. Not if ya wanna stay healthy." It sounded like a warning.

"It's that bad, huh?"

24

"Worse than bad. Three weeks ago Seth Rooney was murdered."

"Really? Do they know who did it?"

"Lightnin' Riders, they call 'em. They come out of the night and hit hard and fast."

"Sounds like vigilantes from the old days," the cowboy said.

"They been knocking off the nesters and ranchers one by one. There ain't but a handful left in the valley now."

"Really?"

"Yes, sir. Look at what happened out there to Callie Dupree at the Circle D."

"What happened at the Circle D?"

"Same as the others. The Lightnin' Riders killed her husband and run off all her cattle. I reckon she's sittin' out there right now at the Circle D, cryin' her heart out. All her cowhands have run off fer fear of gettin' plugged."

"Who's behind all this? Anybody got a reason that you know of?"

Ted chuckled nervously. "Oh, people have a pretty good idea, but they're scared to come right out and say it."

"What about you?"

"I ain't that dumb, either. Best ta keep my mouth shut on that matter."

The cowboy looked at the barman a moment and smiled.

"Yeah, you're right. Best play it safe."

"Those Lightnin' Riders, they all wear masks. Hell, you might be one fer all I know," Ted said, squinting suspiciously.

The cowboy smiled and nodded.

"That's right, Ted, I could be."

Ted stared at the cowboy with a look of uncertainty on his face. There was also a trace of fear in his eyes.

"But I ain't," the cowboy said, laughing.

The barman sighed and smiled.

"Ya had me there fer a moment," he said. "Ya never kin tell." He nodded over to a table where four cowboys drank and played cards. "Hell, all four of them might be Lightnin' Riders, for all I know. Right?"

The cowboy looked over at the table and nodded.

"That's right," he replied. He looked back at the barman. "Say, where is this Circle D you been talking about?"

"What? You goin' out there?"

"Sure."

"What fer?"

"She's short of hands, isn't she?"

"Yeah, she sure is, but you'd have ta be crazy ta walk into thet bear trap, cowboy."

"Well, maybe I am crazy. How do I get there?"

"Well, you take the old coach road west outta town," the barman began. "Ya go ten miles to the crossroads and turn left. It's another five more miles to the south. Ya can't miss it. But make sure ya stay off the Diamond C. It runs up against the Circle D."

"Who owns the Diamond C?"

"Lane Carter. It's the biggest ranch in the valley and he's mighty particular who steps on it. So be warned."

"Thanks," the cowboy said, "I'll remember that."

He finished his food and beer and started out the door.

"What's yer name, cowboy?" the barman called.

"Jared. Clay Jared."

"I'm Ted Norman, Good-luck, Jared."

"Thanks, Norman."

The cowboy named Clay Jared left the Blue Steer Saloon chuckling.

5.

Clay Jared hit the flatlands outside of town at a fast lope then let his dun quarter horse have its head. It ran flat out for a while and when it got that out of its system it settled down to a comfortable, relaxed gait.

Jared turned south on the crossroads and went on for another five miles until a windmill and a white, two-story clapboard house came into view. As he came closer, he made out a barn and a bunkhouse as well. They were down on lower ground in a sort of a bowl surrounded by pines and aspens where a stream ran.

Just as Jared rode through the fence gate, a tall, thin young man, almost a boy, came out of the barn. He aimed a rifle at Jared's chest.

"What the hell you want, mister?"

Jared stayed in the saddle, staring down at him.

"I'm looking for the ramrod, sonny," Jared said.

"Well, thet's me, so what the hell ya want?"

"I'd appreciate it if you pointed that rifle somewhere else, sonny."

"Don't call me sonny," the boy said angrily. "I'm a man, an' I'm runnin' this spread fer Mrs. Dupree."

Jared chuckled and slowly dismounted.

"I didn't say you could git down!" the boy growled.

Two more young men came from the bunkhouse with their guns drawn. They came up close and stared at Jared with interest.

"What-cha got there, Corey?" the mid-sized one asked. He was a bit chubby.

"Nothin' I can't handle, Fern," Corey answered. "You and Mike kin put yer guns away."

"Whatta ya want here, mister?" Mike, the short, stocky one, said.

Jared sized the three of them up and chuckled.

"What the hell's so funny?" Corey asked.

"You. You're all scared like a bunch of rabbits," Jared said, smiling.

"Well, you'd be scared too, mister," Mike said, "if those Lightnin' Riders come at you in the night!"

"Yeah, I heard about them," Jared said.

"Well, you look like you might be one," Fern added.

"I'm not."

"How do we know yer not?" Corey asked.

"You'll just have to take my word for it, boys."

The door of the house opened and there were footsteps on the porch. Jared turned to see who it was. A first glance he thought it was a man but quickly realized it wasn't.

At one time she must have been very pretty. She had the kind of symmetrical face an artist would want to draw or paint. The high cheekbones, straight nose and full mouth were perfectly aligned. Her blue eyes could still grab a man's attention and the abundant auburn hair, tied up in a ponytail, had an attractive, natural ripple to it.

Jared took a moment to study her as an afternoon breeze blew a few strands of loose hair against her wind-burned cheeks. Her mouth was turned down at the corners in a half-pout. It almost made her look like a stubborn school girl.

31

Exposure to the sun and wind had put creases by her eyes but didn't dampen their beauty.

"Can I help you, mister?" Her voice was deep and throaty, yet feminine.

"Ted at the Blue Steer Saloon sends his regards, Mrs. Dupree." Jared said. He suddenly noticed the black armband on the left sleeve of her shirt. "I'm sorry for your loss, ma'am."

"What's your name?"

"Jared, ma'am. Clay Jared."

The tall young man named Corey chuckled. "I had a pig named Clay once." The three of them broke out laughing.

"Now, Corey Drexel, that's no way to speak to a guest," the woman said. It was a mild rebuke said with a half-smile.

"Sorry, ma'am," young Drexel replied.

"Mr. Jared, if it's a job you're looking for I'm afraid you've come to the wrong place. I got no cattle left to wrangle."

Jared chuckled. "Ma'am, I ain't looking for a job. Towns and cities give me a rash. I thought maybe you'd let me feed and water my horse for a few days and sleep in your barn until I get ready to move on. I'm plumb saddle sore and need a few days' rest. I hate to say it, but I'm near flat broke and butt busted at the same time."

Callie Dupree broke out laughing. The three young men joined in. Jared suffered it out, holding his smile.

"Did I say something funny?" he asked with raised eyebrows.

"No, you didn't, Mr. Jared," Callie said. "Come on in for a cup of coffee."

Jared tied his horse to the bunkhouse rail, walked up on the porch and followed Callie Dupree into the house. She took him into the kitchen and he sat at a long plank table while she poured two cups of coffee.

"Ma'am, I take it those three youngsters aren't yours," Jared said.

"You take it right," Callie replied. "No. They ran away from an orphanage in Chicago and hopped a train west to become cowboys. My husband took them under his wing and taught them the ins and outs of ranching, riding and shooting. They're pretty good with a gun but they're too confident."

Jared chuckled. "So I noticed."

"They worshipped Jim, my husband."

"Any idea who these Lightning Riders are?"

"Not really. They're hitting other ranchers, too. The nesters got hit the hardest. They killed Seth Rooney."

"That's what Ted at the Blue Steer told me," Jared said. "How about the Diamond C? Have they been hit?"

Callie Dupree caught the meaning of that question.

"You think Lane Carter is behind the attacks?" she asked with a frown.

"I'm just asking."

"Well, you've got that all wrong. Mr. Carter is too involved in the community to do something like that. He's got too much to lose here. No. You're wrong there. If you ever met Mr. Carter, you'd see what a nice person he is."

"How did he get so big? I understand he's the biggest in the valley."

"He grew his ranch and never broke any laws as I know of," Callie answered. "When ranchers get in trouble with the bank, he's right there to help them. He always offers top dollar for their ranches at foreclosure, and they usually walk away pretty happy about it."

"What about other bidders? Aren't there any other bidders?"

"Sure, mostly outside investors from the East, but the bank gives Carter first refusal."

Jared thought about that for a moment, sipping his coffee.

"Well, then, I guess that lets Mr. Carter off the hook."

Callie stared at Jared and said, "Do you mind if I ask you two personal questions, Mr. Jared?"

"No, ma'am, I sure don't."

"Are you wanted by the law?"

"No, ma'am, I am not."

"Where have you worked last?"

"Down south of here. The Box R, near Caldwell. After that, the Circle C west of here."

"You're one of those cowboys who move around a lot, I see."

"I guess so, ma'am," Jared said, "but I've always been true to the brand, wherever I ride. That's one of the few rules I live by."

"And the other rules? What are they?"

"I'll never refuse to help a lady or a child. I'll never shoot an unarmed man, and I'll always share my food with strangers."

Callie suddenly looked at Jared as if he was an old friend come to visit.

"You can stay in the bunkhouse as long as you want, Mr. Jared," she said with sincerity. "Don't be in a hurry to move on."

"Thank you, ma'am. I appreciate that more than I can say."

After that they made small talk and laughed a lot.

Finally, Jared left and took his horse down to the barn. He unsaddled it, fed it and brushed it down. After putting it in the corral, he stood in the barn thinking.

He had lied to Callie Dupree about being broke. With six months' pay in a secret pocket in his saddlebag, he was in good shape. Jared wasn't sure why he had lied. Maybe he wanted her to think he was down and out and needed help. Whatever the reason, it worked. After getting a look at her, he was glad it did.

He grabbed his saddle and gear and walked up towards the bunkhouse. He'd have to teach those three young cowboys some respect for their elders.

6.

Years ago, while working as a bank manager in St. Louis, Lane Carter became involved with a woman named Nora Castle. When he moved west to invest in ranching, he brought her along with him and presented her publicly as his wife, even though they weren't married.

Nora Castle had his full attention for a few years before Carter spotted a cute young girl who worked at Georgette's Hotel in Thompson Gulch. Her name was Sally Neville, a seventeen-year-old runaway from Helena, Montana. Carter, eager to take pretty Miss Neville off Georgette's hands, arranged for the girl to have room and board at the hotel, which he paid for.

When Nora Castle first got wind of this, she was furious for a long time. But after she calmed down and thought it over, she decided to let things ride as they were. At least for the time being. Let him have his fun for now. She'd have her fun later, when the time was right. Anyway, there were some wild and loose cowboys in the bunkhouse eager and willing to comfort the boss's wife when she needed it.

And when Nora Castle needed comforting, she called on the Diamond C ramrod Dave Larkin do the job.

As for Carter, every Friday afternoon he would ride his buckboard into town to attend the Cattlemen's meeting. He'd chat and drink with the other members for a while and then excuse himself. Under cover of darkness, he would sneak over to Sally's room in Georgette's Hotel. On nights such as that, he never got back to the Diamond C before midnight.

One night he cut the visit with Sally short and went across town to see Stern Addison in his V.I.P. car at the train depot. He planned to meet Stryker there to finalize their plans to kill the owners of the small ranches.

"So," Stryker asked, "when are you going to point out these men to me?"

"Next week at the fundraiser over at the Grange Hall," Carter said. "We'll drop in to make a donation. That's when I'll point them out to you. After that, you'll have to remember their faces and who they are."

"He never forgets a face," Addison said, nodding at Stryker. "I know that for a fact."

"Good," Carter said. After a pause, he added, "But I don't want to be seen with you there."

Stryker chuckled. "Why not?"

"I like to be cautious," Carter replied. "I have a reputation to consider."

"You're a bigshot in town, huh?" Stryker sneered.

"Something like that."

"Don't worry, Carter, I'll pretend I don't know you, if that's how you want it."

"That's how I want it," Carter said coldly. He paused a moment, staring at the gunman. "That's exactly how I want it."

For a moment Stryker looked angry. He quickly recovered and laughed.

"What's so funny?"

"I'm just wondering what's up your sleeve."

"That's none of your business, Stryker," Carter said. "All you have to do is what I tell you, and that's kill them."

"Jesus! You're a cold-hearted bastard, Carter," Stryker said. "What the hell is wrong with you?"

"It's business," Carter replied. "I don't know why you're so bothered about it."

He looked away, avoiding Stryker's stare.

"That's because you don't have to look them in the face when you pull the trigger," Stryker replied.

"Has anyone ever asked you to kill a woman, say, a cheating wife? I'm just curious," Carter asked.

"Yeah, once."

"And did you?"

"Nope. I took the money, shot him and made her a happy widow," Stryker said, dropping his hand down by his gun.

For a moment Carter looked startled. He glanced over at Stern Addison. Addison cleared his throat to break the tension.

"How about a drink, boys?" Addison suggested. He walked quickly to the bar and poured three shots of bourbon.

Stryker smiled, not taking his eyes off Carter. "Sure. Let's have a drink."

Addison passed the glasses around and sat down by Stryker.

"I'd like it better if you two got along," Addison said, "Okay, Stryker?"

Stryker shrugged and smiled.

"Sure, boss. Whatever you want," Stryker said, laughing sarcastically.

He already hated Carter's guts.

7.

The Grange Hall was a large barn set in the middle of a field just off the old coach road, about a mile west of Thompson Gulch. By sundown the field was packed with carriages, buckboards and horses. The wide double doors were open to let the breezes in, and men walked around outside smoking and chatting in the summer air.

Carter drove his buckboard off the road and found a spot near some scrub oaks to tie up. Stryker rode past him and tied up a few yards away. He dismounted and walked several feet behind Carter, following him into the barn. There was a door fee of a quarter eagle.

A man in a suit collected guns inside near the door. He hung them there on a wall peg. Stryker handed his over and walked on, stopping a few feet away to look around.

There were several tables set up against the wall to Stryker's left. At one, women sold homemade cakes, pies, jams and jellies. At another table, they sold jars of pickled vegetables and homemade cheeses.

Near these tables were benches where men, women and children sat. Many of the children were releasing their energy by chasing each other around the empty dance floor in the middle of the room.

Straight ahead, against the back wall, was a raised plank platform. Three men, one with a banjo, one with a violin and one with a mouth-harp, stood there waiting for a command to start playing.

To Stryker's right was a makeshift wooden bar on barrels. It was amply stocked with locally made beer, hard cider and homemade wines and whiskeys. Carter walked over to it. Stryker waited a moment then went over and stood beside him. Carter ordered a glass of hard cider and Stryker ordered a glass of plum wine.

Suddenly Carter noticed a big bear of a man standing to his left. The man held a drink and was a bit unsteady on his feet.

"Mallory!" Carter said loudly to be heard above the crowd. "How are you, sir?"

Carter held out his hand. Mallory ignored it.

"Where's yer asshole railroad friend, Carter? I'd like ta kick both yer asses!" Mallory said.

The man next to Mallory turned and grabbed his arm.

"Come on Frank," he said. "Leave the bastard be. He'll get his someday."

The two men walked away into the crowd. Carter waited until they were out of earshot and said without looking at Stryker, "That's Frank Mallory and Dan Riley. I want them taken care of first."

"Any others around?"

Carter looked around, then faced the bar again.

"See that skinny one with the white Stetson over by the cake table? That's Phil Bishop. And the short one with a red shirt over by the musicians. He's Bob Sanders."

"Okay. Is that all of them?"

"There's two more, but they're not here as I can see."

Suddenly, an elderly man carrying a water pail walked up near the musicians on the platform. He stood in front of them and set the pail down. Everyone seemed to have been waiting for this and stopped talking.

The man cleared his throat and said, "Hi, everybody, and welcome to the Grange Hall. For those of you who don't know who I am, I'm Arnold Bedloe, Grange Master and manager of the Granger Savings and Loan in town."

A few people yelled out a greeting and Arnold Bedloe nodded, smiling.

"Tonight," Bedloe said, "we're going to have a dance auction. We're going to raise money so that Seth Rooney's widow and children can pack up and go back home to Colorado. You all know what happened to poor Seth."

A sympathetic murmur rippled through the crowd.

Mr. Bedloe looked to his right where a group of eight women in Sunday dresses stood waiting. He nodded and they walked up on the platform and stood in a row to the left of him. He stared at them for a moment and then smiled back at the crowd.

"Now you bachelors and widowers out there, this is your chance to do a really good deed and get to dance the rest of the night with a pretty girl as well. And you can't beat that, can you? No, you can't."

He waited as the unattached men edged in closer to get a look at the women.

"So, dig deep, men, and let's get the bidding started. And remember, you only get to dance with 'em, not keep 'em!"

The crowd laughed and the woman nearest to Mr. Bedloe took one step forward.

"Miss Charlene Purdy!" Bedloe said loudly.

The bidding for Miss Purdy started at three dollars and ended at ten. The winner, a young farmer, dropped his money in the pail and led his prize to the middle of the dance floor where they stood side by side, waiting for the bidding to end.

The auction quickly resumed with Mr. Bedloe making humorous remarks for the enjoyment of the crowd. In the group were women of every age, size and shape, including widows and divorcees.

"For you lonely widowers out there," Mr. Bedloe chuckled, "here's your chance to connect with a seasoned woman."

The bidding amounts rose and fell and finally the last woman stood awaiting.

"Folks, our final volunteer is widow Callie Dupree," Bedloe called out with enthusiasm. The last word had no sooner left Mr. Bedloe's mouth when someone shouted out a bid.

"Six dollars!"

"Twelve dollars!"

"Fifteen dollars!"

The bidding went rapidly higher and higher. When it reached twenty-five dollars there was a long pause. Mr. Bedloe looked around and waited, hoping to stretch it out higher. Just as he was about to call it a done deal, someone over by the bar yelled out.

"Fifty dollars!"

Arnold Bedloe wasn't sure he had heard right.

"What? Did someone say fifty dollars?"

"Hell, if you're going to argue, make it a hundred!"

"A hundred?" Bedloe strained to see who it was.

"That's right, a hundred!"

The crowd turned in surprise, gasping in awe as Stryker shouldered his way through. He walked up to Mr. Bedloe and flipped five gold double-eagles into the pail. They rang as they hit bottom and bounced around. The old gentleman looked down into the pail and then smiled.

Stryker ignored Mr. Bedloe and held out his hand to Callie Dupree. She had a look of wonder as she stepped down on the dance floor and stared up into Stryker's face.

"Who are you, mister?" Callie asked.

"Stryker, Ed Stryker, ma'am. And may I say you are the loveliest woman in the room."

"You're a smooth talker, Mr. Stryker," Callie said, smiling.

Before Stryker could reply, the band started to play "Alabama Jubilee". The dancers formed a circle and started the dance. Mr. Bedloe's voice rang out.

> *"In and out twice, allemande,*
> *Do-si-do and move on!*
> *Allemande back, to partner swing.*
> *Promenade and move on..."*

After that came the "Belfast Duck". Mr. Bedloe's rich voice rang out against the rafters where lanterns hung, shedding their light down on the dancers.

> *"Form a circle, then lead*
> *And chasse down!*
> *Ditto up and ditto down,*
> *Duck through an arch..."*

Callie and Stryker danced a while then stopped on the sidelines to catch their breath.

"Let's wait for the slow ones," Stryker said.

"Alright," Callie answered. She was awed by this handsome man.

As if reading Stryker's mind, the band leader announced it was slow dance time and the band started into a waltz. Stryker led Callie back out onto the floor, took her in his arms and held her close. She put her head on his shoulder and closed her eyes, letting herself be swept away across the floor.

For Callie, it came to an end all too soon. They stood on the sideline again, their eyes locked onto each other's faces.

Stryker was hypnotized by Callie, unable to look away. She smiled up at him, enjoying his full attention.

Finally, he said, "I have to go now, Mrs. Dupree. It has been a rare pleasure."

"Likewise, Mr. Stryker."

For a moment he didn't move. Then Stryker smiled and walked away. Callie watched him go, wondering who he was, where he came from and where he was going. Arnold Bedloe walked up to her and put a hand on her shoulder.

"I'm glad you decided to come, Callie," he said. "That hundred dollars will help a lot. Who is he?"

"His name is Ed Stryker," Callie said.

"Do you know him?"

"No, I never saw him before, Mr. Bedloe."

"He's quite a ladies' man, isn't he?"

Callie nodded. "Yes, he is. And a real gentleman."

Outside, in the glow of lanterns hanging from the trees, Carter stopped Stryker by his horse. He was angry.

"You damn fool! I told you to lay low. Now they've all seen you."

Stryker tightened the saddle cinch.

"So what? They don't see any connection between us."

Carter was seething, almost boiling with anger.

"I called you in here and you'll do as I say! I'm paying you to kill, not make love!"

"Maybe I'll do both," Stryker replied.

He mounted up and rode off into the night, chuckling.

8.

Lane Carter came into the V.I.P. car, poured himself a drink at the bar and sat down facing Stern Addison. He didn't look happy.

"This Stryker," Carter said, "He's not taking this thing seriously enough. And I don't trust him."

"Don't worry. When he gets the job done, he'll be gone and you'll own every ranch in the valley."

"Have you been reading the newspaper?"

"Yeah, but it doesn't mean anything. As soon as the Rooney woman goes, she'll be quickly forgotten. That's how they are, those peasants," Addison smirked. He was feeling superior today.

"I'm not so sure about that," Carter answered.

"Well, you had your man Larkin kill her husband, so it's your worry. Don't complain to me about it."

"Where's Stryker?"

"He said he was going for a ride in the country to get the lay of the land."

Carter pulled a cigar from his jacket and lit it.

"I bet he's going out there."

"Out where?"

"To the Circle D. The Dupree spread."

"Why would he do that?"

Carter chuckled. "The damn fool danced for hours with her at the Grange Hall. I think he's taken an interest in her."

Addison scowled. "You worry too much, Carter. He uses women. She won't mean anything to him."

At about that same moment, Stryker was fifteen miles away with his horse on a rise, overlooking the Circle D ranch house. Staring down, he saw what appeared to be five men working on a corral fence. He finished a cigarette and rode slowly down through the open gate and into the yard.

No one seemed to hear or notice him as he dismounted and tied his horse at the bunkhouse rail. He walked quietly down to where the men were working.

"Where's your remuda?" Stryker asked.

54

They all wheeled around in surprise. Stryker raised his hands and chuckled.

"Don't plug me, boys. I'll hand over the cash!"

Suddenly he saw that one of the cowboys was a woman.

"Is that you, ma'am?" Stryker asked with a surprised look on his face. He tipped his hat.

"Yes, it's me, Mr. Stryker, calluses and all."

Stryker chuckled. "Well, ma am, I have to say you sure do a lot for those cowboy clothes. And I mean that in a good way. You make a mighty fine cowgirl."

Young Fern Scully scowled. "What the hell you want, mister? You sellin' Bibles or somethin'?"

Callie Dupree hit him with a stern look.

"Calm down now, Fern, Mr. Stryker is paying me a social call, is all."

"That's true, ma'am," Stryker said.

"This is my crew," Callie said and introduced the boys. When she came to Jared she stopped a moment to carefully choose her words. "And this is my new hand, Mr. Jared."

Stryker stared hard at Jared for a moment. "Darn if you don't remind me of somebody!"

Jared chuckled. "Did we have fun?"

"We sure did," Stryker said, nodding. "It was a long, long time ago. We were young and crazy!"

"Well, it wasn't me, sorry to say," Jared replied.

"Yeah, I guess not."

"I would have remembered," Jared said.

"An' he'd a remembered you too, pig breath," Corey Drexel chuckled.

Before Jared could reply, Stryker took up his cause.

"Kid," Stryker said, "you have a bad mouth on you. Better keep it in check."

Drexel puffed his chest up like a rooster on the attack.

"Who says, mister?"

Callie stepped in. "Right now would be a good time for you boys to go over to the bunkhouse and play cards."

The three young men nodded and went slinking away.

"Mr. Stryker," Callie continued. "Would you care for a cup of coffee?"

"I'd love to, ma'am."

Callie led Stryker up to the house. Jared stood alone like the last man on earth. He sighed, leaned against the corral fence, slowly built a cigarette and lit it. He stared up at the bunkhouse and smiled. When he was finished smoking, he crushed out the butt with his heel.

"It's lesson teaching time," Jared muttered and headed up the yard to the bunkhouse.

Once inside, Jared unbuckled his gunbelt, dropped it on his cot and walked over to the table where Drexel, Scully and Perry were playing matchstick poker.

"What was that remark about my breath, sonny-boy?"

Drexel smirked confidently and stood up, facing Jared. "I said you had pig's breath, is what I said. You wanna make something of it, asshole?"

Drexel never saw it coming. Jared drove his left fist into his belly. As he folded in half, Jared swung his other fist in a roundhouse right that connected with the young man's jaw.

Drexel dropped like a rock on the floor.

"You rotten sonofabitch!" Fern Scully yelled.

As Scully and Perry came at him, Jared danced to the side and clubbed Scully behind the ear. He went sailing over one cot and onto another. He didn't get up. Perry got a good punch in on Jared's jaw, but it wasn't good enough. Jared hit him flush in the nose, breaking it. Perry's head seemed to explode. He saw stars and sat down on a chair, holding his face. Blood gushed between his fingers.

"Hold your head back, kid," Jared said. "It'll stop bleeding quicker." He sat down at the table and shuffled the cards. "Anyone feel like a friendly game of poker?"

Nobody answered.

Later, after Stryker had left, Callie called the others in for coffee. By then Perry's nose had stopped bleeding, but it was a black and blue mess.

"What happened to your nose, Michael?" Callie asked.

"He broke it," Perry whined, pointing at Jared.

"Did you break his nose, Mr. Jared?"

"Yes, ma'am, as I recall, I did break Mr. Perry's nose."

"May I ask why?"

"You may ask that question, ma'am."

"Well, I'm asking it, then."

"Well, Mr. Drexel, Mr. Scully, Mr. Perry and me, well, we had a little dispute, sort of."

"What was it sort of about, Mr. Jared?"

"It was sort of a pecking order dispute, ma'am. You know what that is, don't you?"

"Yes, Mr. Jared, I have heard about such disputes," Callie replied. She looked at the bruises on the other two boys. They sat quietly, saying nothing. "By the looks of it, it appears you came out on top."

"It appears that way, ma'am."

"And it's all settled and done with, I hope?"

"I'm sure it is," Jared said, holding back a smirk.

"The reason I called you all here is to tell you that tomorrow morning we're going to ride out to check the line shacks to see what shape they're in," Callie said. "Is there any question about that?"

No one said a word.

"Good, then," Callie said, "let's have some pie."

"Is he comin' around here agin?" Fern Scully asked.

"Mr. Stryker? I don't know. Perhaps. Why?"

"Well, I don't like the way he looked at you, ma'am," the young man said.

"That's because you're not a woman, Fern," Callie said.

Jared chuckled and grinned. Callie gave him a hard look.

Early in the morning they took a packhorse with extra water, jerky and hardtack and started out for the west line shack. On the way there they saw only a few stray cows and one or two yearlings.

"Somebody has cleaned you out pretty good," Jared said.

"Yes," Callie replied sullenly. "The Lightning Riders."

"They must be working for someone with an interest in the valley. Otherwise it doesn't make any sense."

"That might be," Callie replied.

"Do you suspect anyone?"

"No. It have no idea why they did it. It just doesn't make any sense."

They rode on.

The Circle D was not all that big a spread. They came up on the west line shack in three hours. Two hours after that they hit the north shack. They stopped there to eat and rest the horses. There was good grass there and a stream. Cottonwoods dotted the area, their pale green leaves shining in the afternoon sun.

They went on and reached the east line shack late afternoon, then headed back in. They had counted not more than three hundred stray cows. The land around them was breathtakingly beautiful. Green, rolling hills and slopes and fields of wild rye and wheat grass stretched for miles, red and gold in the fading sunlight.

The Circle D spread was prime land with plenty of water. Even though a few mountains of rock cut into it, it was, for the most part, a carpet of green with low, rolling hills. It was an ideal place for raising cattle.

"It's beautiful," young Fern Scully said.

"I'd fight for this," Mike Perry admitted.

"Yeah, so would I," Corry Drexel affirmed.

They were tired when they rode into the yard of the Circle D long after sundown. After taking care of the horses they put them in the corral. The boys went into the bunkhouse while Jared and Callie sat on the porch drinking coffee.

"So, what was all that about, ma'am?" Jared asked.

"I wanted a last look before the bank takes it out from under me," Callie said. "I've lived no other place but here all my life. My parents are buried out back, by the hill."

"It's that bad then, is it?"

"Yes. It's that bad," Callie said. Suddenly she got up. He couldn't see her face in the dark but he sensed she was near to crying. "I have to go in now, Mr. Jared. Goodnight."

After she went in he sat on the porch a while, thinking about how rotten life could be. She was a fine woman and didn't deserve this.

Something had to be done, and maybe he had to do it.

9.

On Monday mornings, Young Mike Perry would usually drive the buckboard into Thompson Gulch with Callie Dupree sitting beside him. It made him feel important. In his mind he was protecting her.

When Dave Larkin, ramrod of Lane Carter's Diamond C, learned of this, he decided to have one of his men test the kid's quick-draw skills. So, one Monday morning after sending out the work details, Larkin and a few of his special cowhands dropped in at the Blue Steer Saloon for a couple of drinks. Once he was there, he stationed a man on the porch to let him know when the Circle D buckboard arrived. He and the other men stayed inside to have a drink or two.

Larkin had a mean side as well as a sadistic sense of humor. His idea in messing with the young Circle D cowboy was to throw a scare into Callie Dupree so he could brag later to his boss, Lane Carter, about it. Plus, after this, she'd be short another cowhand. Maybe she'd sell out like Carter wanted. She was one tough nut to crack. They had hit her hard and she was still standing.

"She's comin', boss!" The Diamond C lookout called into the Blue Steer. "Her an' that punk kid, the short, stocky one, Mike Perry. The one that looks like he lost half his brain when he was born."

Larkin chuckled and turned to the man on his left at the bar.

"Bart, you think you kin take the kid?"

Bart, a tall, ragged, lean cowboy with a scar on his left cheek and bushy eyebrows, chuckled.

"Christ, yes. Any day a the week an' twice on Sunday."

"Then go do it," Larkin said.

"Ya want me ta jest wing the kid or plug him?"

"Put one between his eyes. That should scare hell out of the rest of them. Maybe it'll send them running."

Bart nodded. "Yeah. It jest might do thet."

Bart tossed down what was left of his drink, checked his gun and walked out on the porch of the Blue Steer Saloon. He looked down the road at Meek's Mercantile. The young cowboy, Perry, had just come out with a stick of hard candy in his hand. He stood leaning back against the mercantile, chomping away.

Bart chuckled again and walked down towards him.

"Hey, kid," Bart said as he approached the platform where Perry stood. He noticed the patch over the kid's nose. "Looks like you got kicked in the face by a mule. Did you have yer face too close to its ass? Haw!"

"Very funny," Perry replied.

"You work fer thet Dupree woman, don't ya?"

"Yeah," Perry replied, "I work fer her. What about it?"

"I hear she's easy. Is thet right, kid? Is she as easy as they say she is?"

Mike Perry glanced down at Bart and then up at the Blue Steer Saloon. He saw the Diamond C ramrod with three men staring back at him. It quickly dawned on him what was going on and he smiled.

"You work fer thet shithead Lane Carter, don't ya, asshole?" Perry sneered.

Bart stiffened. His eyes narrowed and he lowered his hand down by his gun, taking up the stance. The kid had a sharp tongue. All of a sudden it didn't seem like the kid was all that stupid.

"What did you jest say, kid?"

"I said, you work fer shithead Lane Carter and yer a Diamond C asshole."

Bart's face turned purple with rage. The muscles in his jaws rippled as he clenched his teeth.

"Kid, yer dead," he growled. "You jest don't know it!"

Bart went for his gun but never quite got it clear of the holster. Mike Perry's hand became a blur as he drew with lightning speed and shot the Diamond C cowboy square between the eyes. Bart's head snapped backwards and his legs turned to rubber as he whirled around and fell smack down on his face in the road.

When Larkin saw that things had backfired on him he shook his head.

"Damn!" he said. He turned to two of his other men. "Ed, you and Larry go down there and drill that little sonofabitch!"

Just as the Diamond C men rushed down towards the mercantile, Clay Jared rode at a slow canter up the main street of town. When he saw the two men approaching Perry, he pulled up to Callie's buckboard and dismounted. He walked up near Ed and Larry and looked down at the body lying near the steps of the platform.

"What's up, Mike?" Jared said, sizing up the Diamond C men.

"I'm havin' me a shindig, Jared," the young cowboy said. "You want in?"

"Sure," Jared said.

Ed and Larry turned to stare at Jared.

"Who asked you ta butt in, mister?"

"The kid did," Jared said. "Didn't you just hear him?"

"Hell," Larry chuckled. "Sure. If ya feel froggy, jest jump on in."

The people of the town who had seen the shootout between Perry and Bart gathered nearby to look on. Mr. Meek, owner of the mercantile, and Callie came out on the loading platform to watch.

"What's going on?" Mr. Meek asked.

The one called Ed pointed to Bart's body.

"Thet kid done bushwhacked my pal here, an' he's gotta answer fer it."

"Is that true, Mike?" Callie asked.

"Heck, no, ma'am," Perry replied. "I was jest standin' here mindin' my own business when thet darn fool came up an' braced me for no reason at all."

The one called Larry cracked the knuckles of his gun hand. His body sort of danced back and forth nervously.

"Come on down here in the road," Larry said. "You're gonna pay up fer what ya done ta Bart. He was my pal an' I can't let it stand."

"Sure," Perry chuckled. "Hell, I ain't afraid of you, mister. Or yer buddy there."

"We'll see about thet, kid," Ed replied.

Larkin watched with keen interest from the saloon porch. He felt confident Ed and Larry would finish the kid off. They were his two fastest men. But this other one, the intruder, who the hell was he to be sticking his nose in where it didn't belong?

Larkin chuckled. No matter. Ed and Larry were fast on the draw. It was the stranger's tough luck.

Some people, aware of what was about to happen, quickly took shelter wherever they could find it. Others stayed.

Mike Perry walked slowly down from the loading dock to join Jared. They walked a few yards up the road together and stopped.

Jared said, "This should be about right, kid."

"Whatever you say, Jared." Perry didn't seem to be too concerned. He was more preoccupied with his stick of candy than anything else.

They turned to face Ed and Larry. Jared stood a few feet to the left of Mike Perry.

"You sure?" Jared asked. "You want to get closer?"

Perry tucked the stick of candy into one cheek and said, "Nope. This is fine."

"You gonna shoot and chew candy at the same time, kid?" Jared asked.

"Yep," Perry said, cool as a cucumber.

"Good luck with that, kid," Jared said.

Perry nodded. He looked down the road and saw that Ed was facing Jared and Larry was facing him.

"Hey, mister! Yer a sheep-lovin', pig-kissin' asshole!" Mike Perry yelled at Larry.

They all drew.

Larry was fast and fanned off two shots at young Perry. But the kid wasn't there. He had crouched low and stepped to the right before Larry fired. Both shots were off their mark, although one did rip a hole in the kid's shirt by his left arm.

The young Circle D cowboy fanned one shot off into Larry's heart. The Diamond C cowboy's body flew five feet backwards and lay sprawled on the ground.

Ed, at the same time, went for Jared's head. The bullet took Jared's hat off but missed flesh and bone. Jared, with legs bent and back straight, fanned off two shots so fast it sounded like one. Both shots slammed like a sledgehammer into Ed's chest. He did a weird dance, fired his gun into the ground and fell on his face in the road.

Mike Perry holstered his gun and took a bite of his candy stick. He looked at Jared and said, "You were a little slow."

Jared nodded and picked up his hat. He sighed. "Yeah, I guess I'm getting a little too old for this, kid."

"Here comes the law," Perry said.

The town marshal came rushing on the scene from an alley.

"What in tarnation is going on here?"

"Hi, Fred," Mr. Meek said. "Glad you got here."

"Hi, George," the marshal said back. He looked at the three bodies. "God Almighty! Who did what to who here?"

"Those men on the ground are Diamond C men, Marshal Sloan," Callie said. "I'm afraid they braced my men and lost. Mr. Meek and I saw the whole thing from the doorway."

"That's right, Fred," Mr. Meek said. "We saw the whole thing."

Dave Larkin came down from the Blue Steer Saloon with two men towing their own horses and those of the three dead men behind them.

"Marshal," Larkin said. "I'll take 'em, if ya don't mind."

"Alright," the marshal said. "Tell Mr. Carter I said hello."

"Sure thing," Larkin replied dryly. After he and his men tied the three bodies on the horses, he tipped his hat to Callie Dupree. "Good afternoon, ma'am." He stared hard at Jared and Perry. "I'll be seein' you two agin."

"Any time," young Perry sneered. "Only the next time send somebody who can shoot straight, Larkin. This was too easy."

Larkin and his men mounted up. He gave the kid a cold stare and left with the bodies in tow.

Jared looked at Perry. "Kid, you just can't behave yourself, can you?"

Perry took a bite of his candy stick again and chuckled.

"I ain't had this much fun since me an' some friends of mine overturned ol' man Porter's outhouse. An' he was in it at the time, too."

"You're plumb crazy, kid," Jared said. "Then, maybe not."

He slapped Perry on the back and they shook hands. Callie looked on, shaking her head in disapproval.

Yet, she had a feeling of pride. Mike Perry had defended himself and her honor quite skillfully. And so had this stranger, Clay Jared.

Suddenly she felt very secure. More secure than she had felt in a long time.

Maybe there was hope, after all.

10.

Lane Carter saw himself as a highly respected pillar of the community, much loved and admired by the people in the area. In Carter's mind, Stryker was a crude gunman, a nothing. Stryker was stupid while Carter was intelligent. Carter was high-born and educated while was Stryker was not.

But, worst of all, Stryker's attitude was intolerable.

After spending restless hours at night thinking about how to teach Stryker who was boss, Carter came up with an idea for putting Stryker in his place.

He drove his buckboard down to the railroad to see Stryker at the V.I.P. car. When he got there he went directly to the bar and poured a drink.

Stryker, who was sitting in a chair reading the local newspaper, looked up in surprise and then chuckled. That irritated Carter.

"What's so funny, Stryker?" Carter asked.

"Nothin'," Stryker replied with a smirking look.

Carter looked around the car.

"Where's Addison?" he asked.

"He's in the back room."

"Go get him. Tell him I'm here!" It was more a command than a request.

"He's busy, whatta you want?"

Carter took his drink to a chair and sat across from the gunman.

"Alright, since you asked, I want that stupid woman dead by tomorrow."

Stryker was confused for a moment then it settled in who Carter meant.

"She wasn't on your list," he said.

"She is now. I'm putting her on it."

"Haven't you done enough to her already? You had her husband killed and then ran off all her cattle. Isn't that enough? She's got no money and no cowboys. What the hell else do you want from her?"

Carter enjoyed seeing Stryker on the defensive, squirming like a worm on a hook.

"I want you to kill her. That's what I hired you to do, kill whoever I told you to kill!"

Stryker thought a moment. "Our deal was I get paid by the head, like a bounty hunter."

"That's right. A thousand a head and I'm putting a thousand on Callie Dupree's head."

Carter smiled. He knew he had Stryker cornered. The gunman stared coldly at him.

"I'm passing that one up," Stryker said. He put the newspaper aside.

"Why? Does she mean something to you? Are you interested in her?" Stryker looked away, avoiding Carter's sneering look. "I thought so. I knew it when I saw you two dancing at the Grange Hall. You're hooked on her."

Stryker jumped up out of his chair with his fists clenched.

"Shut yer face, Carter, or I'll smash it in!"

Carter smirked. He was enjoying the moment. He had penetrated Stryker's shield and made him lose his temper.

The man was no longer the cool, cold killer but a lover defending his woman.

"Or you'll what, kill me?"

Stryker looked confused for a moment. He finally got control, sighed and sat down again.

"I won't do it," he said bluntly.

"Then I'll get Addison to hire somebody else to do it."

At that moment Stern Addison came out of the bedroom pulling up his suspenders. His face was flushed and he looked exhausted. He walked to the bar and poured a drink. After knocking it down he poured another.

"What the hell is all the shouting about?" he asked.

"Your man refuses to do what he's told, Stern," Carter said, then chuckled. "Maybe you should talk to him."

Addison took a chair between Carter and Stryker. He looked at the gunman.

"What's the problem, Ed?"

"He wants me to kill Callie Dupree. I won't do it."

"Why not?" Carter cut in.

"Because it's against the code. You've been here long enough to know that, Carter. It's a hanging offense. You don't kill women out here. It ain't like Chicago or St. Louis."

Addison sipped his drink and looked at Carter.

"He's right, Lane. And you know it. He'd be a fool to kill her."

"I'm from Chicago, Stern," Carter said. "I don't hold all that much to the code. Anyway, you do hang women out here for stealing cattle, so how about that?"

"Callie Dupree is no cattle rustler, you sonofabitch!" Stryker exploded. "I ought to drill yer carpetbagger ass right here and now!"

"Hold it, Ed!" Addison yelled as Stryker dropped his hand down alongside his gun. "Let me talk to him alone."

Stryker's gun hand was shaking. He inhaled deeply and pulled himself together. He nodded to Addison.

"Alright, you do that, boss. I'm going up to the Blue Steer Saloon. The air doesn't stink as much up there and the company is better."

Stryker stomped out of the car, started across the tracks for town but suddenly stopped and looked back. He stood as if undecided, which way to go, then walked swiftly but quietly back to the car. He stood up against it with his ear next to a window, near enough to hear clearly what Addison and Carter were saying.

"Why the hell did you have to throw it in his face, Lane?"

"I wanted to see him twist in the wind and he did."

"You are one sadistic bastard," Addison chuckled. "You haven't changed one bit." He sipped his drink. "Hell, if you really want that Dupree woman out of the way, you should have come to me."

"Okay," Carter smirked, "I do and I am."

"Alright," Addison said. "I'm bringing in some specialists. The way you're doing it, this one-by-one with Stryker is too slow. We've got to get this taken care of fast as we can so I can make an offer to the railroad moguls for running that spur through."

"Specialists?" Carter asked. "Isn't that a bit heavy?"

Addison chuckled. "Maybe, but when they get finished with those nesters and small ranchers, this valley will look like a cyclone hit it. They'll come in here like the hounds of hell and be gone in one night. This place won't know what hit it."

Carter imagined it as Addison spoke.

"Beautiful! Great! Then all our problems will be over!"

"Exactly," Addison said. "They'll chop this place up in little pieces."

"To the real Lightning Riders," Carter said, raising his glass in a toast.

They finished their drink and Carter stood up to leave.

"Leaving so soon, Lane, old buddy?" Addison asked.

"Yeah."

"Going to see Sally, are you?"

"No," Carter said. "I only see her on Fridays. You know that."

Addison chuckled. "Oh, yes, that's right. I forgot,"

As Carter left, Stryker crouched and ran around to the other side of the car and watched him head for his buckboard up by the train depot.

Stryker smiled. Sally Neville was in the back room of the V.I.P. car. She had been there all the time.

Stern Addison was cuckolding his good friend, Lane Carter, and Carter didn't even know it.

There was no honor among thieves.

11.

Stryker knew what Carter and Addison were up to. It was simple. Addison would bring in a dozen hired guns disguised as Lightning Riders to sweep the valley clean. They would ride in, finish off the farmers and small ranchers and disappear like the wind. The law would never touch them.

When the raid was over, Carter would step in to help the surviving widows and children. He'd offer to buy up their land at a fair price and would be seen as a savior in the valley. Addison, too, might step in and give the survivors free train passage to wherever they wanted to go and be seen as a man with a heart.

Carter and Addison would be heroes. They had it all figured out. So did Stryker, and he didn't like it.

He also thought Addison was thinking of getting rid of him, too. Maybe he was winding up his career with the railroad and was looking to make one last money-making deal with Carter. From all indications, that's what it looked like.

After his argument with Carter in the V.I.P. car, Stryker rode out to the Circle D. He met Clay Jared by the corral.

"Look, Jared," Stryker said, "I don't know you, but I take it you care what happens to Callie Dupree."

"Sure," Jared said, rolling a cigarette. "Why? What's up?"

"Carter and my boss Addison mean to hurt Mrs. Dupree real bad."

"How bad is real bad?"

"Like killing her bad," Stryker said.

Jared handed Stryker the makings.

"Thanks," Stryker said and began to build a smoke.

"How do you know this, Stryker?" Jared asked.

"I heard it with my own ears."

Jared stared at Stryker.

"You did, huh?"

"That's what I said, didn't I?"

Jared nodded and thought for a moment.

"I've heard about Carter, but who the hell is this Addison fellow?"

"He's the agent for the railroad in this area."

"How do you know so much about him and Carter?"

Stryker chuckled. "Because I'm connected to the railroad."

"How, if you don't mind my asking."

"Let's just say I solve problems whenever something or somebody gets in its way."

"You're a hired gun, is that it?"

"You could say that."

"And Carter and Addison are after Mrs. Dupree?"

"Not only her, but all the nesters and small ranchers as well. Addison and Carter are aiming to wipe out the whole valley, then step in and take ownership of it."

"That sounds a little crazy. How do they aim to do that?"

"Addison is bringing in a dozen riders dressed up as Lightning Riders."

"Can he do that on his own?"

"If he wants to," Stryker replied. "The big shots in Houston don't keep an eye on him all that much. All they want are results. And he usually gets results, one way or the other."

"I see," Jared said. "Thanks for letting me know, friend."

"What are you going to do about it?" Stryker asked.

"First thing is to tell Mrs. Dupree," Jared said.

"Let's do that right now, then."

They went up to the house. Callie greeted Stryker and took him and Jared into the kitchen for coffee.

"What brings you out our way, Mr. Stryker?" Callie asked. "Seeing the sights?"

"Well, it's a bit more than that, ma'am," Stryker said. "I wanted to let you in on something important."

"Well, I'm listening."

Stryker told Callie the same story he had told Jared. She listened carefully, nodding. Her face became intense.

"What can I do about it, Mr. Stryker? Is there anything I can do?"

"Nothing, I'm afraid," Stryker said.

"What if I told the town marshal?"

"It's too big for him," Stryker said. "You'd need a small army to handle this. Do you have a small army, ma'am?"

Callie Dupree laughed.

"An army? Where would I get an army, Mr. Stryker?"

They fell quiet for a moment then Jared said, "I think I might know where."

Callie looked at Jared in surprise. "You do? Where?"

"When is the next Grange meeting?" Jared asked.

"Tonight, come to think of it. Why?" Callie asked.

"I think you and I should go and talk to them. After all, it involves them as much as you, ma'am. See if they want to fight for their land."

"That might work," Callie said. "It's worth a try."

"What time is the meeting?" Stryker asked.

"Six tonight," Callie replied. Then, "You're putting yourself in a bad position, Mr. Stryker. How come?"

Stryker shrugged. "I've done some things for the railroad, ma'am, but they never asked me to gun down helpless women and children."

"What exactly was your job with the railroad?" Callie asked.

"Hunting down train robbers and troublemakers," Stryker said.

"That must be dangerous."

Stryker nodded. "It can be. Some people I come across are fast on the draw. It's always a question of how fast."

They were quiet for a moment. The gunman stood up and smiled at Callie.

"Thanks for the coffee, ma'am." He turned to Jared. "I'll be going back to town now. I'll try to find out when Addison is calling in these men. When I do, I'll let you know."

"If we're not here, we'll be at the Grange Hall," Jared said.

Callie studied Stryker's face for a moment. "Thank you, Mr. Stryker."

"Call me Ed, and don't mention it, ma'am," he said and left.

In an hour he was back at the V.I.P. car talking to Stern Addison. The railroad man started lecturing him.

"If you're going to work for Carter, you had best learn to let him run the show, Stryker," Addison said. He pulled a cigar from his lounge jacket and lit it.

"I'm through with Carter," Stryker said. "We don't see eye to eye."

"Oh, really? I'm sorry it didn't work out."

"Yeah, me, too."

"So, you're going back to Hays City, then?"

"Unless you've got something for me to do. I'm itching to do a little real gun work again. It's too damn dull around here."

Addison stared at Stryker trying to figure out if he was serious.

"You want real action?" he asked Stryker. He gave Stryker a hard look.

"Sure. I'm always looking for real action."

"Maybe I can give you all you want, Stryker."

"Really? Doing what?"

"Leading an attack on the valley. I've decided to bring in some Regulators. Carter doesn't know what he's doing."

"You want me to ramrod them? Why me?"

Addison slowly pulled a cigar from his coat and lit it, all the while staring at Stryker.

"Because I know your reputation for getting the job done and doing it right. They'll need a smart leader. I'd like you to be that leader."

Stryker nodded. "You know I don't work cheap."

"You get the job done in one night and you'll get five thousand flat out. Only there's one more thing."

"What's that?"

"Leave Carter out of this. Make sure you don't touch his spread."

"Why not?"

"When it's all over people will notice that his place wasn't touched. They'll wonder why."

"I see. They'll think he had a hand in it."

"That's right. They'll tar and feather the damn fool and run him out of town on a rail.

"Why hang him out to dry?"

"Because I have a plan and it doesn't include Carter," Addison said. "I just figured out that I don't need him to get what I want. In fact, he's only in my way."

"Does it include her? The girl?"

"She's part of it, yes, but only a small part."

Stryker laughed hard. "You're a slick one, boss."

Addison smiled and blew cigar smoke towards the ceiling.

"I know," he chuckled, "I know!" Then, "There's a meeting at the Grange Hall tonight. Why don't you drop in and see what it's all about, then report back here?"

"Sure, good idea." Stryker started out but turned back. "Say, boss, when and where do I hook up with the Regulators?"

"Next Monday. Midnight. Behind the water tower in the field behind the depot. The leader's name is Harker."

"Harker?"

"Yeah, Harker. Tell him I sent you to lead the attack. Make sure they don't touch Carter's place. Is that clear?"

"Clear as a bell, boss," Stryker said.

After he left, Stryker went over to the Blue Steer Saloon and stood at the bar, thinking. He thought about his line of work and that it was a dead end. Dealing with men like Carter and Addison was beginning to make him feel dirty.

When he met Callie Dupree he knew he'd have to change. She was worth changing for.

12.

Callie Dupree and Clay Jared were already at the Grange Hall when Stryker arrived. Promptly at six in the evening a man took the podium and called for order.

A woman read off the minutes of the last meeting and several farmers and ranchers made announcements. They talked about events such newborn babies, birthdays, weddings, deaths and items for sale.

Finally, a half hour later, Mr. Bedloe took the podium.

"Anyone else have anything important to say?" he asked.

Callie Dupree stood up and raised her hand.

"Callie, you got something to say, do you?"

"No, Mr. Bedloe but Mr. Jared does."

Jared stood up alongside Callie Dupree.

"And who might you be, Mr. Jared?" Mr. Bedloe asked.

"I work for Mrs. Dupree."

"Oh, since when?"

"About three weeks or so now."

"You've only been here three weeks and you already got something to say?" Mr. Bedloe asked to the amusement of the crowd. They roared with laughter. When it died down, Mr. Bedloe said, "Well, let's hear it then, young man."

Jared waited a moment then said, "I'd ask everyone to look at the person next to you. Do that now, if you would."

Murmurs and chuckles went through the crowd of about sixty people, most of whom were family members. Others were friends and neighbors.

Jared waited a moment, then said, "If there is a stranger next to you, grab him and bring him up here."

A man near the back broke out through the crowd and ran for the door. Several men went after him but came back empty handed. The man had gotten clean away.

"What in tarnation is going on here?" Arnold Bedloe asked. He was a little bit shaken and confused.

People in the crowd began talking to each other while others milled excitedly about. Mr. Bedloe called for quiet but got none. It was as if a bunch of old hens had gotten loose and were running wild. They were completely out of control.

Suddenly a shot rang out. Jared saw Stryker holding his gun high and waving it. The crowd froze and stared at him. Many recognized him as the man who had danced with Callie Dupree at the fundraiser.

"Shut the hell up, you idiots," Stryker yelled. "Listen to what the man is saying or you're all gonna die!"

The crowd suddenly got very quiet.

"Callie, who was that man who lit out like a scared rabbit?" Mr. Bedloe asked.

"I don't know," she replied.

"He was most likely a spy for Carter or Addison," Jared said.

"For Mr. Carter? Mr. Addison?" Bedloe asked. "Why, that's crazy! Why would they be spying on us?"

Callie told them what she had learned from Stryker. When she was finished, she realized it sounded wild and crazy. She knew right away that they didn't believe her.

A farmer stood up. "Thet don't sound like Mr. Carter or Mr. Addison to me. Why would they be spyin' on us?"

Most in the crowd agreed.

Another joined in. "Mr. Carter has helped lots of us. And as fer Addison, he's got no reason ta be watchin' us."

"I'd trust Carter any day of the week," another rancher added.

Then someone called out to Mr. Bedloe, "What about you, Arnold? What do you think?"

"Yeah, Mr. Bedloe, whatta you think? Is it true?"

Mr. Bedloe scratched his chin and sighed.

"Well, if you're asking me, I'd say I don't rightly know. But supposing what Callie said is true? What then?"

There was more murmuring from the crowd.

"Even if what she says is true," another rancher said, "what can we do about it? The old marshal can't do anything. Hell, he ain't even got a deputy."

"I say we have a special meeting ta talk this thing over," someone said. "Just us men. In the back room. The women an' children kin wait out here."

A vote was taken and it was decided that the women and children would sit around talking, drinking cider and eating cake while the men took the matter under consideration in the back room.

Callie waited patiently for almost an hour. Finally, the meeting was over.

Jared and Stryker came out of the back room with the others and walked over to Callie where she sat with a rancher's wife. She saw the look on their faces as they took her aside.

"They don't believe us, do they?"

"One or two did, but not the rest." Stryker replied.

"I guess there's not much we can do, then, is there?" Callie asked.

"Not that we can think of right now," Jared replied.

The three of them mounted up and rode back to the Diamond C where Drexel, Scully and Perry met them in the yard. They all went in the kitchen for coffee.

"What's the next move?" Callie asked.

Jared shrugged. "I guess there's nothing we can do except practice our fast draw."

13.

There was a time when railroads were the targets of choice by criminals of every kind imaginable, from pickpockets to small and large gangs. Passengers rode in fear of being robbed, and mail cars carried armed guards. Since the trains carried everything from cattle and tobacco to silk and gold and traveled across lonely stretches of land, they were easy targets waiting to be taken down. With over 20,000 miles of railroad track, the West soon saw the birth of the special western outlaw called the train robber.

Railroads also had another vexing problem, and that was strikers who banded together and took up arms against the workers who stayed on the job. Many a bloody battle erupted and people were wounded and killed as a result.

In order to put a stop to these constant attacks, the railroads decided to fight fire with fire. They hired men for their ability to shoot a gun, regardless of their past lives. If they were criminals, they got pardons from various state governors to work for the railroads. The railroads were suffering losses in the millions of dollars and it had to be stopped.

One answer was men like Ed Stryker, once a train robber himself but now a highly paid defensive weapon working for the railroad.

Stryker's job was to track down and infiltrate certain gangs of robbers and strikers and neutralize their leaders. With his reputation as a train robber it was easy to do. He became very good at this dangerous job and earned a reputation as the man to go to when you wanted things done quickly and neat.

When Stern Addison heard about Stryker, he sent for him under false pretenses, telling his superiors that he needed Stryker to infiltrate a gang of train robbers operating in his area. Of course there was no such gang, but Addison's bosses didn't know that. They sent Stryker to do a job different from what Addison had proposed.

Once Stryker realized this, he figured he'd keep quiet and see where it went. When Carter told him what the job was, Stryker, at first, had second thoughts. Then he considered doing it for a thousand dollars a head and go back to Hays City a rich man.

That is until he met Callie Dupree and became aware of her situation. When he saw what Carter had done to her he decided to kill him. He hated him like he had hated no other man.

Stryker already was seeing a split between Carter and Addison. Neither one trusted the other. In fact, it seemed they were beginning to detest each other more and more each day.

And it wouldn't be long before Carter found out that Sally Neville was cheating on him with Addison.

In truth, Stern Addison was ready to double-cross Carter and go on his own. He was tired of the rancher's superior attitude, of his constant bragging about what a respected man he was in Thompson Gulch. That would soon come to an end if Addison's plan with the Lightning Riders worked out.

And now Stryker would see that it did.

A few years ago, a man named Jim Gary was an agent at Thompson Gulch. When Addison came to replace him, Gary took Addison aside and handed him a piece of paper with a man's name on it. The man's name was Harker.

"What's this, Jim?" Addison asked.

"If you ever get tangled up in a mess or a strike, or need a special job done where it takes a lot of men, send a wire to this man at the Clarendon Hotel in Hays City. Mention my name. Harker works cheap, doesn't ask questions and he's not particular about the job. Give him a couple of days to get here and he'll come."

"How do you pay him?" Addison asked.

"Out of the contingency fund. There's always more than enough in it for emergencies."

Addison chuckled. "This Harker, he's sort of a Regulator, is he Jim?"

"Yeah but Harker isn't his real name. It's just the one he uses. He mostly works with a dozen or so men, all from the other side of the law. I've used him a few times to break up strikes and he's good. But the railroad doesn't know about him. It's best to keep it that way."

Gary told Addison that Harker and his men would jump at the offer of a few hundred dollars each. After all, they were nothing but cheap, hired killers.

In his wire, Addison specified the place Harker would meet him to get the details of the job. It was in a field by a water tower near the Thompson Gulch train depot on a certain Monday at midnight.

Soon he, Addison, would be the shining knight in Thompson Gulch. Carter would be in deep trouble, and sweet little Sally Neville would be his.

But as in all plans, what can go wrong usually goes wrong.

Sally's ardor for Carter was fading. He noticed this, and in time he began to have suspicions that she might have a secret lover on the side. The very thought of it ate at him like a dull pain. One day, the rancher made a move. He had his ramrod Larkin plant spies everywhere in town, especially in the Blue Steer Saloon and at Georgette's Hotel to keep an eye on Sally Neville.

When Carter finally learned his suspicions were true, that Sally spent the evening hours at the V.I.P. car every night except Friday, which was when Carter visited her, he went into a rage. He beat his fists against his chest and moaned like a wounded animal. He even got drunk. Finally, he decided to take revenge. It was time to show Stern Addison he was no fool.

One Thursday evening at nightfall, the rancher drove his buckboard into town and tied up at Georgette's Hotel.

He met the spy in the lobby.

"She's over there in that fancy railroad car with Addison, boss."

Carter gave the man a double eagle, told him he didn't need him anymore and sent him back to the Diamond C. He then got in the buckboard and drove it over to the railroad depot a hundred yards away. After tying up at the rail there, he walked quietly another fifty yards to the V.I.P. car.

Approaching from the back room end, Carter stopped. His face turned purple as he listened to the sounds within. The curtains were drawn and the lights were out. The longer he listened the more he began to shake with rage. Veins bulged in his head and he clenched his teeth in anger.

Carter swore under his breath, walked quietly but quickly up the length of the car to the other entrance and went slowly in.

An oil lamp on one of the tables shed a soft glow. The rancher went to the bar and poured a drink. He knocked it down in one gulp. He drank two more and held the empty glass in his hand, staring at it. Suddenly he bellowed like a bear and flung the empty shot glass down the other end of the car. It smashed against the back room door, shattering with a loud bang.

"Addison, you scoundrel," Carter roared, "come out here and meet your maker! You conniving, backstabbing bastard!"

"Is that you, Lane?" It was Sally Neville's voice. She sounded terrified.

"Yes, Sally, you whore! It's me! Come out here so I can whip your ass!"

There was a short silence.

"Alright, darling," Sally finally replied, her voice shrill and trembling with fear. "Just give me time to put some clothes on, honey." There was a pause. "I'm sorry, Lane. I know I've been a bad girl. I'll be good. I'll never cheat on you again, darling."

"Oh, don't worry about that, baby," Carter yelled. "When I'm finished beating your ass it won't make any difference if you're good or bad because you'll be dead! Dead, do you hear me? Dead!"

"Please don't be angry, Lane, darling."

"Stop talking and get out here, Sally! And you, too, Stern." He waited a moment. "Did you hear me, Addison?" He got no answer, so he said, "Come on out Addison and we'll talk it over. I'm a reasonable man. It's not your fault. She made a play for you, didn't she?"

Carter drew his gun, aimed it at the bedroom door and fanned off three shots.

"Did I hit you, Stern? I hope so."

Carter heard a body hit the floor with a thudding sound.

"No, you dumb bastard! You just killed Sally!"

Lane Carter suddenly realized Sally Neville had been stalling for time. Addison was behind him. As Carter whirled around Addison shot him with a New Line derringer from two feet away. The force of the .32 caliber bullet knocked Carter backwards into a chair.

"You sneaking bastard." Carter sputtered.

Addison shot him again, in the chest. The big rancher grunted from the impact, then smiled.

"That peashooter ain't nothing but a toy," the rancher growled as he thumbed off a round into Addison's heart. The force of the much bigger .45 caliber bullet drove Addison sailing out the door and over the railing. He fell sprawled on the ground between the railroad tracks.

Carter sat in the chair staring ahead with dull eyes. His breathing was forced and shallow and blood bubbled from the corner of his mouth. He tried to get up but couldn't and sat back in the chair. His grip on the gun relaxed and it fell to the floor. Finally, Carter's eyes saw nothing and he stopped breathing.

Outside, up by the train depot, someone's dog gave out a mournful howl.

14.

Arnold Bedloe lived above the Granger Savings and Loan bank. On Monday night, he lay in bed tossing and turning. Ever since the meeting a day ago at the Grange Hall, he had been haunted by what Callie Dupree's ramrod, Clay Jared, and the man called Stryker had told him. If what they said was true, then bad things were going to happen, and soon.

In one hour it would be midnight and all hell would break loose in the valley.

Just the remote possibility of the truth made him fear for the worse. In his mind's eye he visualized those men, dressed as Lightning Riders, sweeping across the valley burning and killing, destroying farms and ranches.

And he could do nothing.

The awful thing was, not one of the farmers and small ranchers believed it was going to happen and weren't prepared to defend themselves. They weren't prepared because they refused to believe it was possible that Lane

Carter and Stern Addison were evil men. Even Bedloe himself found it hard to believe. As for the marshal, no one even bothered that old man with this unbelievable, nonsensical story.

As for Jared and the man called Stryker, they were seen as intruding outsiders who were misleading Callie Dupree. They had no business coming in here and spreading false lies about two of the most trusted men in the valley, Mr. Carter and Mr. Addison.

The old man tossed and turned with worry. It was all in God's hands, anyway, not his, he thought. If it did happen in an hour, only a miracle could save them. At that moment he was glad he wasn't married. It would be an unfit thing for a woman's eyes to see.

Suddenly he heard horses walking past the bank. He went to his bedroom window and looked out into the street. It was that man Jared again. With him were Stryker, Callie Dupree and her three young, reckless ranch hands. One still had the bandage on his broken nose.

Mr. Bedloe watched them ride towards the train depot. He looked at his watch. It was a quarter to midnight. He sighed and went back to bed. He said a prayer for Callie Dupree.

Out in the street Jared had glanced up at the window above the bank. He saw the curtains move and knew it was Mr. Bedloe. He quickly turned his attention to the deserted street ahead. The town was completely empty except for a stray cat sitting on the porch of Meek's Mercantile. When it saw them it ran and hid.

They rode strung out side-by-side, keeping some space between them. Jared and Stryker were a few feet out in front.

They moved slowly past the Blue Steer Saloon, the mercantile and the stable. After turning right at the Cattlemen's Association building, they crossed the tracks behind the train depot. The lights were still on in the telegraph office. The telegrapher was reading a magazine.

When they came to the V.I.P. car they saw Addison's body at the passenger's end. They dismounted and tied their horses to the platform railing. Stryker knelt by his boss's body to see if he was still alive.

"He's dead," he told Jared and Callie.

Jared took out his Colt and cautiously went into the car. The rest followed. For a moment it looked like Carter was asleep in the chair with his head down, his chin on his chest. The blood told the story. He, too, was dead.

They heard a moan from the bedroom and saw the bullet holes in the door.

"It's Sally Neville," Stryker said. "We'd better go get the doctor."

"I'll go," Callie said. "He lives close by."

As Callie rushed off on foot, Jared checked his pocket watch.

"What time is it?" Stryker asked.

"It's almost midnight."

"We have to go."

"Alright," Jared replied.

They hurried from the V. I. P. car. Once out on the tracks, they walked over to the nearby water tower and into a stand of pine trees. On the other side of the trees was a small field. Twelve hooded men sat on their horses, waiting under the faint, pale glow of a quarter moon.

Stryker, Jared and the three young cowboys stopped about thirty feet in front of them and slowly dismounted.

"Is that you, Mr. Addison?" the leader of the group said in a low voice.

"No, I'm Stryker."

"Where's Mr. Addison?"

"He's dead. Who are you?"

"I'm Harker. Yer lyin' about Addison. He ain't dead."

"I'm afraid he is, friend."

"Who killed him, you?"

"No, a man named Carter."

Harker whispered to the man on his left, then turned back to Stryker.

"I don't know anyone called Carter and I don't know you, either, Stryker," Harker said. "What the hell is going on here?"

"Like I said. Addison is dead and it's called off," Stryker repeated. He slowly dropped his hand down by his gun. Jared and the others did the same.

Harker turned to the man on the left and whispered again. Finally, he turned back to Stryker.

"Yer sayin' Addison's dead and it's off?"

"That's right. It's off."

"Addison was supposed to pay us five hundred each for a night's work. It was a long ride down here. We ain't leavin' unless we get paid."

"There's no raid and there's no money," Stryker said.

"Then we'll just take Addison's strongbox with us," Harker said.

"What strongbox?"

"The one they keep in that V.I.P. car."

"That's railroad property," Stryker said.

"We'll take it anyway," Harker replied.

"I can't let you do that."

Harker looked at Stryker and chuckled.

"It's twelve to five. I don't see how you can stop us."

"Take your men and leave," Stryker said again.

"And what if we don't?"

"Then you'll all die here."

Harker broke out into a laugh.

"Who have you got with you, Billy the Kid?"

"No," Mike Perry said calmly, "he's got us."

Perry drew and shot Harker out of the saddle.

Jared went into a crouch and fanned off three shots. Stryker, next to him, fanned of another four. The Regulators, caught up in their saddles, were unable to get off clean shots as their horses shied and bucked. Gunfire rang out in the black of night. Gasps and groans and the sound of bodies crashing to earth echoed all about. Horses shrieked and ran off with empty saddles, their hooves pounding, fading away with the barking of the last gunshot.

No sooner had it started than it was over. There was a strange silence.

"Anybody hurt?" Jared asked. His left arm was bleeding.

"I took one in the right leg," Perry said. "Not too bad, though."

"Shit, my right ear lobe is gone," Fern Scully whined. "The girls ain't ever gonna look at me agin!"

"I got grazed in the ass," Drexel groaned.

"How the hell did that happen?" Scully asked. "Was you runnin' away scared?"

"I don't know," Drexel replied. "Maybe it was 'cause I was a-shootin' sideways, sorta." They all chuckled nervously.

Suddenly they heard a groan. Stryker was kneeling on the ground a few feet away. It was hard to see in the dark, but it looked like he had a hand to his chest.

"He's been plugged!" Fern Scully yelled.

They ran over to Stryker. Jared knelt next to him. They could hear his shallow breathing. He leaned against Jared.

"Bad?" Jared asked.

Stryker tried to chuckle but couldn't. Finally, he just nodded and said, "Yeah."

Jared looked over at Corey Drexel. "Go get the doc. He's probably in the railroad car. Hurry!"

"Forget the doc," Stryker whispered. "One of those bastards got in a lucky shot. I'm done for." The gunman coughed. "Just let me lay down."

"Go, kid!" Jared growled at Drexel. Drexel ran off into the night.

Jared eased Stryker backwards onto the ground. He looked up at Jared and sighed.

"The earth is cool. Feels good," Stryker whispered. Jared could barely make out his smile in the darkness. "Hell, I can't complain. I did my share of killing, too." He coughed harder this time. His body shook from the effort, forcing a groan. "Callie Dupree, isn't she something?"

"She sure is," Jared replied.

"She's the best dancer..."

Stryker's body shuddered and a long, soft sigh pushed up from his chest. His head turned against the earth and Jared knew he was gone.

Suddenly people came running into the field from the direction of town. Some carried lanterns. Others carried guns and rifles. When they saw the bodies some gasped in horror. Others muttered to each other. The marshal broke through. He was half-dressed and carried a scattergun.

"Alright, what happened here?"

"Look, Marshal," a woman shouted, "those men over there! They're all wearing hoods!"

"They're the Lightnin' Riders!" someone yelled.

There were nine bodies lying in the grass. Six horses milled about at the edge of the field. The other six were nowhere in sight.

"Any of them alive?" the marshal asked.

"Here's one!"

"Here's another one!"

Jared and his group slinked through the crowd and limped back to the V.I.P. car. Callie was there with the doctor. He was bent over the body of Sally Neville. Corey Drexel and Callie walked over to Jared.

"You still want the doc?" Drexel asked.

"No" Jared replied.

Callie stared at him. She looked about to cry. "Mr. Stryker, is he?" Callie asked.

"Yes," Jared replied.

Callie Dupree walked toward the door.

"He's dead, ma'am," Jared said.

"I have to see him," she replied and left.

The doctor shook his head and stood up. He stared down at the body of Sally Neville.

"She's gone," he said. He saw the condition of the others and nodded. "You all line up and I'll tend to you."

Jared went to the bar and poured a shot of whiskey. He wanted to be alone for a while. In a few minutes Marshal Sloan came in. He walked up to Jared.

"What the hell is Addison's body doin' out there on the tracks?"

Jared shrugged, took a drink and shivered it down.

"Where's the one called Stryker?"

"He died out there, helping us," Jared said.

"One of them raiders died cursing him all to hell," the marshal chuckled. He looked at the slight wounds the men had and nodded. "Nice job. This valley owes you an' those boys a debt of gratitude."

"What did the other one say?" Jared asked.

"He babbled somethin' about Addison hiring them to wipe out the farmers and small ranchers. But he died, too.

Lucky, two of the townsfolk heard his confession." Suddenly the marshal noticed Carter's body. "What the hell! Is thet Carter over there, dead in thet chair?"

"Yeah," Jared said. "It looks like Addison and him tangled over Sally Neville. That's her body over there. She just died."

The marshal glanced over at the girl's body and groaned. "Christ Almighty! All three are dead? Am I going crazy? What the hell is going on here?"

"Have a drink, Marshal," Jared said. "It's on the railroad."

He poured Marshal Sloan a drink.

15.

Two days after the shootout in the field behind the water tower, two articles appeared in *The Thompson Gulch Valley Star*. The first article read:

"On Monday last, just after midnight, citizens of Thompson Gulch awoke to the sound of gunfire coming from a field near the old railroad water tower east of town. By the time Marshal Sloan arrived at the scene the shooting had stopped. Nine hooded gunmen lay dead on the ground. Apparently, they were Lightning Riders.

Four cowhands from the Callie Dupree's Circle D Ranch and a man called Stryker had met and stopped them in a fast-draw shootout. The Circle D cowhands suffered minor wounds but Stryker died in the gunfight."

The article went on to say:

"The Marshal said the hooded men were Lightning Riders who came here to attack the farmers and small ranchers. Who was behind them is not known at this time."

Below that article was another one, which read:

"The bodies of rancher Lane Carter, railroad agent Stern Addison and Sally Neville were found in a lone railroad car near the train depot on the same night that the bodies of the Lightning Riders were discovered. It's unknown what happened, but speculation and rumor has it that the two killed each other in a duel over Miss Neville. It appears that she was accidently caught in the crossfire."

A week later, another article appeared in the newspaper that read:

"When the properties of deceased rancher Lane Carter went to court for adjudication, it was discovered Mr. Carter had left no Last Will and Testament. The court also denied Carter's companion, Miss Nora Castle, had any legal claims on Carter's properties."

It ended with:

"An announcement will be published in the area newspapers inviting all legal claims on Mr. Carter's estate. If none are made within sixty days, the Carter estate will fall under the control of the county."

A week later, another article appeared that read:

"A new railroad agent has arrived in Thompson Gulch to replace the late Stern Addison. His name is Vern Gilchrest. Mr. Gilchrest says his mission is to improve relations between the railroad and the farmers and ranchers of the area. Arnold Bedloe, head of the Granger's Local, said that Mr. Gilchrest had better do that or he would be facing a lawsuit. It appeared that two citizens of Thompson Gulch had heard one of the dying Lightning Riders confess that Stern Addison, the previous agent, had hired the Lightning Riders to wipe out the small farmers and ranchers. Speculation has it that Mr. Addison had a plan in mind that involved the railroad and the land in this area. The details of that plan are not yet known."

A few days later, a final article appeared covering the Lightning Riders and the railroad.

"This newspaper has received an anonymous letter that claims to explain what has been going on in this area for the last year or so. According to the letter's author, rancher Lane Carter and railroad agent Stern Addison were scheming to take control of all the land owned by the nesters and the small ranchers in our valley. When this was accomplished, Addison would convince the railroad to build a spur across the land to the cattle town of Larchmont Springs.

However, the two men turned on each other over the charms of beautiful young Sally Neville, whom, it was discovered, that Carter was keeping on the side at Georgette's Hotel. When Carter discovered that Miss Neville was sharing her considerable charms with Mr. Addison, the two men had a deadly confrontation and killed each other, as well as Miss Neville."

After a flurry of articles, the newspaper lost interest in Carter, Addison and the entire Lightning Riders matter.

16.

When the ramrod of the Diamond C, Dave Larkin, learned about the death of his boss, he wasn't disappointed. In fact, he licked his lips like a hungry wolf staring at a lamb. His cowboys had been culling cows out of the small ranchers' herds for years. They had them hid at the far north end of the Diamond C spread, in a place only they knew about.

Not being the type to sit idle, Larkin gathered his little army in the bunkhouse for a parlay. All sixteen of them.

"Men," Larkin said, "the boss is gone and good riddance to the stingy bastard. The county will most likely break the Diamond C spread up into sections and sell them off to the highest bidder. You all have seen it done before."

Larkin paused to roll and light a cigarette.

"Now is the time ta make a move while there's confusion going on. We got about sixty thousand head of shorthorn beeves tucked away in the north valley. I say we split them up into three herds of twenty thousand each and head 'em fer Mexico an' sell 'em."

"When do ya wanna do that, boss?" someone asked.

"I was thinkin' like right pronto, maybe tomorrow."

Larkin stopped there and waited for any remarks.

"What about her?" someone asked, nodding towards the ranch house. "Where's she headin'?"

"She's pullin up stakes and headin' back ta Chicago where she came from."

"How do you know thet?" someone else asked.

"Because she told me so," Larkin replied.

A wave of laughter rippled through the bunkhouse. They all suspected that Larkin and Nora Castle were playing games on the side. Larkin took the laughter with a smile.

"You an' her are cinched pretty tight," Tom Springer, second ramrod, chuckled.

Larkin smiled and said, "Yeah, we sorta are." Then he turned serious. "When we leave, we're gonna take everything we kin, even the horses in the corral. We'll turn some of them inta packhorses and load 'em with food and gear."

"What about the larder, boss?" the cook asked. "It's full of fancy canned grub and salted meats."

"Take whatever ya fancy, Cooky," Larkin chuckled. "Just so long as we eat good." The men nodded in agreement over that last remark. "Anybody got anything ta add?"

Larkin waited but no one said anything.

"Alright, then. Let's git it all packed tonight," he continued. "We'll leave early in the morning. It's a four hour ride if ya go straight at it. An' if the weather's good, we'll be there by noontime."

He pointed to Springer, his assistant ramrod.

"Tom," he said, "yer in charge of gettin' everything ready ta go in the mornin'. Have Cooky and two others help."

"Me, boss?" Springer replied sourly.

"Yeah, you, an' don't give me no back talk."

"Well, whatta ya gonna be doin'?"

Larkin smiled. "I'll be busy sayin' my last goodbyes to a certain lady."

"Ya need any help with that, boss?" someone yelled.

"No, boys, I kin handle this bronc all by myself."

The boys laughed as Larkin left and headed towards the ranch house.

"I guess the boss likes his women big," someone in the group said.

That brought more laughter.

"Well, let's git her done!" Springer yelled.

The following morning at sunup, Dave Larkin led his caravan out of the Diamond C yard and headed north. Sixteen men and ten packhorses followed behind him. Nora Castle did not bother to come out and wave goodbye and Larkin never bothered to look back. She was somewhere in the house packing her clothes.

Larkin thought she might be crying, but she wasn't. As a matter of fact, she was smiling.

She had been preparing for this day from the start. To secure her future, she had been saving the spending money Carter gave her each week, and whenever he came home drunk on Friday nights from his meetings with Sally Neville, she took money from his billfold. He never caught on and always suspected it was Sally Neville doing the stealing.

Miss Castle had quite a bankroll tucked safely away in her bosom. She would quickly forget Carter, but not Dave Larkin. He was a wild and crazy lover. Something Carter never was.

17.

Larkin started his men out at a slow pace at first so as not to put a strain on the heavily loaded packhorses. But in an hour he picked up the pace and got them moving faster, riding across broad fields of whiskey grass and wild rye.

Tall cottonwood trees dotted the landscape alongside fast running streams. Their leaves shimmered and sparkled in the sunlight. Stands of birches stood in groups like sentinels dressed in dirty white uniforms. High above, a pale blue sky packed with clouds reached to the far horizon. Birds flew in flocks and, higher up, eagles soared on the currents.

Time after time they passed small herds of Diamond C cattle. There was no one to attend to them. They were on their own now.

Four hours later, they came to an opening between two high hills in the north end of Diamond C land. They stopped a moment to look around then rode in. Half a mile on and they came to a barbed-wire fence with a gate. Two of Larkin's men dismounted and swung the gate open for the others to ride through. When the last packhorse went by they closed the gate again and caught up with the others.

Farther in, the valley shaped into a huge oval of wild wheat and rye grass. The land dipped lower here, and cattle grazed in the lowlands near a wide stream of sparkling water.

The Diamond C cowboys rode down a rise, dismounted and let their horses rush down to the stream to drink. There was a small lean-to by a large cottonwood near the stream.

"Over there, men," Larkin yelled, pointing. He walked through the tall grass, pointing in the direction of the lean-to. "We'll build camp there. We kin rest for a couple of days an' then head the herd out fer Mexico."

Suddenly, one of the cowboys pointed back up the rise and yelled to Larkin. "Hey, boss, we got company!"

They all turned at once to see four riders walking their horses slowly over the rise towards them.

"Who the hell are they?" someone asked.

"Looks like Jared and them three snot-nosed kids from the Circle D spread," another said.

Jared, Drexel, Scully and Perry stopped about twenty feet away and put their hands on their saddle horns.

"Howdy, Larkin," Jared said. "Nice day, ain't it?"

"You got some nerve ridin' in here, just the four of you." Larkin chuckled. "You won't be gettin' out alive, ya know."

"How many head you got here, Larkin?" Jared asked.

"It ain't none of yer business, but we got sixty thousand or more, why?"

Jared smiled. "Because we're taking them all is why."

"Takin' 'em all, you say?" Larkin looked at Jared, laughing. "You're plumb crazy, Jared. I got sixteen guns a-pointin' at you right now."

Jared nodded, raising his eyebrows. "Hell, Larkin, that ain't nothing. I got thirty men with guns and ropes." He raised his arm as a signal.

"The hell you have," Larkin said with a sneer. "Yer bluffin'. Kill 'em all, boys!"

But the Diamond C men didn't draw. They stood frozen as a large band of men came riding over the rise straight at them.

"You didn't think we'd come alone, did you, Larkin?" Jared chuckled.

Callie Dupree led a small army of cowboys from the various small ranches down the rise. As she rode up alongside Jared, the others spread out in a row, their rifles pointed at the Diamond C men.

"Hello, Mr. Larkin," Callie said calmly. "Nice day for a hanging."

Larkin sneered. "Okay, Mrs. Dupree, what's the deal?"

"Ask Mr. Jared," Callie replied. "It's his party."

Larkin shrugged and looked over at Jared.

"Whatta ya got in mind, Jared?"

"Well, I'll tell you what, Larkin," Jared said, "you and your men just head on out for Mexico, and the herd stays here. It's as simple as that."

"How about lettin' us have half?" Larkin asked.

"Not likely," Jared chuckled. "You rustled every one of those cows from Mrs. Dupree and the other small ranchers. That's a hanging offense and you know it. That's why we brought the ropes."

Springer shifted nervously in the saddle. "Hell, Larkin, let 'em have them. I ain't gonna do a rope dance over no stolen beeves."

129

All of the Diamond C men nodded.

"That settles it then," Springer said.

He started to walk his horse around the intruders when Callie Dupree raised a hand.

"Hold it," she yelled. Then, in a level voice she said, "No one is leaving until we find out who killed Seth Rooney!"

"And Mrs. Dupree's husband, Jim Dupree!" Jared added.

"You want one of us ta squeal?" Larkin asked.

"Call it what you want," Jared cut in. "One of you better start talking and quick!"

"An' if we don't?" Larkin said with a sneer.

Jared quickly answered, "Then you'll all hang right here. Every damn one of you. Your bodies will rot out here and no one will ever find you. You and your men should think about that, Larkin."

The Diamond C ramrod suddenly didn't look so confident. He looked around at his men and then pointed at Springer.

"Springer did it. He killed Jim Dupree!" Larkin said.

"You squealing sonofabitch!" Springer yelled and went for his gun.

Larkin saw it coming and drew. He was faster and shot Springer in the heart. Springer's body flipped backwards over the cantle and hit the ground with a thudding sound.

"There," Larkin said. "Thet solves that problem. Let's go, men."

None of the Diamond C cowboys moved.

"I said, let's go, men!"

One of the cowboys said, "Thet was a dirty deal ya jest pulled on Springer, boss. It wasn't right. Springer wouldn't never a squealed on you like thet."

"Shut yer mouth, Red, or I'll shut it fer ya!" Larkin yelled.

He turned his gun on the cowboy called Red.

"He did it, Mrs. Dupree," Red said, pointing a finger at Larkin. "It was the night we raided the Rooney farm. Rooney came out shootin' at us and Larkin drilled him."

"You bastard!" Larkin shouted.

"Put it away, Larkin!" Jared said. "The game is up."

The Diamond C ramrod's face turned red with rage. He stared quickly around at everyone, then moaned.

"You ain't gonna hang me, ya sonsabitches!" Larkin yelled. He put his gun to his head and pulled the trigger. His head snapped sideways and his body toppled to the ground.

Callie Dupree closed her eyes and looked away. The cattle down by the lake raised their heads to look up and then went back to grazing. For a moment no one knew what to say.

Jared finally spoke up. "It's time to go, boys," he said. "Hit the trail or talk to the rope."

The Diamond C cowboys walked down to the lake to get their mounts and packhorses. Jared and a dozen cowboys escorted them up to the valley entrance then stopped and watched them go. When they were satisfied, they rode back to the others.

"We'll stay here tonight and leave in the morning," Jared said. "When we get near the Circle D, we'll stop to separate the brands."

"We should bury Mr. Larkin and Mr. Springer," Callie said.

"We'll do that," Jared replied.

He formed up a burial detail and they went to work digging the graves.

Later, in the evening, Jared and Callie Dupree walked down to the lake and stood by a pine tree watching the sun settle slowly behind the mountains.

"It's a miracle," she said. "I was finished, done for, and now I've got my herd again."

Callie stared at the westering sun, deep in thought as Jared rolled a cigarette.

"Mr. Stryker. He was a strange man, wasn't he?"

"Yeah," Jared answered. "He was half good, half bad."

"I liked the good part," Callie said. "I never noticed the bad."

"He felt special about you."

"Oh? Did he?"

"Yes, his last words before he died were, 'She sure was a good dancer.'"

Callie smiled. "Really?"

"Yes."

"Well, he was a good dancer, too," Callie replied. Then, "What about you, Mr. Jared? Are you a good dancer?"

"Tolerable, ma'am. Tolerable."

"At the next Grange dance we'll see, won't we?"

"Yes, ma'am, we sure will."

They stood quietly watching the sun go down.

The End

Other western books by R. Annan

Fight for the Lazy M
The Red Bandana

Jack Cordell Westerns

The Gunfighter in Winter
Long Ride to Hell's Kitchen
Owl Hawks
Gunfight at Barfield Springs
Shootout at Sanctuary City
Last Days of a Gunfighter

Clay Jared Westerns

Copperhead Moon
Cowboys of the Box R
Prisoners of Brimstone Pass
Range War in C Minor
Devil Wind
Showdown at Wamego Falls

Coming Soon: Jesse Garnett Westerns

Coming Soon: Cody Brent Westerns

About the Author

R. Annan is a seasoned and traveled author with many interests. As a career serviceman, he served in Korea and Vietnam. He also completed a one-year course at the Defense Language Institute at Monterey, California, and graduated from the University of South Florida with a B.A. in Art and Art History. After taking a two-year course in screenwriting at the Hollywood Scriptwriting Institute, he established The Old Time Radio Club Time Machine as both a scriptwriter and an actor.

As a young boy growing up in the city, R. Annan never passed up a chance to see a western movie. His heroes were Buck Jones, Johnny Mack Brown, Wild Bill Elliot and John Wayne, to name a few. As an adult, he often wondered where his love of westerns came from. Perhaps it has something to do with his grandfather, John L. Annan, who was a cowboy from Helena, Montana, in days of old.

A Note from the Author

Thank you for reading my book. If you enjoyed it, would you please consider rating and reviewing it? I'd enjoy your feedback. Thank you!